Wildcat
Summer

❦❦❦

Mary Riskind

❦

1985
Houghton Mifflin Company Boston

With love to Paul, whose interest in bobcats
began this story, and to Reba, without whose
constant lap-sitting and purring it might
have been completed sooner, but not so warmly

And special thanks to Megan, Tim, and Steve

Library of Congress Cataloging in Publication Data

Riskind, Mary.
  Wildcat summer.

  Summary: While vacationing in the country, two city
children start a complex chain of events when they
find a litter of abandoned kittens and determine to
take care of them, not realizing they are bobcats and
cannot be taken back to the city.
  1. Children's stories, American. [1. Bobcat—
Fiction.   2. Grandmothers—Fiction.   3. Old age—
Fiction.   4. Country life—Fiction.]   I. Title.
PZ7.R493Wi   1985   [Fic]   84-22573
ISBN 0-395-36217-2

Printed in the United States of America

S   10   9   8   7   6   5   4   3   2   1

1

❧❧❧

Vicky paused in the entrance to the summer house, letting the loose-sprung door nudge her from behind. The floor was a checkerboard of missing tiles, and bright blue paint on the cupboards was chipped and peeling. She pressed the handle of the water pump standing next to the doorway. The squeals made goose flesh rise on her skin.

"Give me a hand, will you?" Skip hollered through the screen. He was dragging his suitcase and a shopping bag overflowing with model airplane kits.

"It's your own fault. If you hadn't brought so much, you wouldn't need help."

As he let himself in, Skip bumped the bag, and pieces of white plastic scattered everywhere. Vicky had warned him to put rubber bands around the boxes, but he was too dumb to listen. He never finished any of the kits. That's why they were pieces instead of airplanes.

Vicky left Skip moaning over his mess and poked her head around the corner to the living room. The small writing desk and the maple-leaf lampshade her mother found at the Wolfeboro Fair were pushed aside in a warren of carelessly stacked bookcases. A daybed with a tie-dyed cloth for a cover had been added. Probably it came from the Wolfeboro Fair, too.

When her grandmother died, Vicky's mother and her

two uncles decided to keep the New Hampshire cottage until all the grandchildren were grown. At first there had been problems scheduling who could have it. Now it was a question of who had the time to drive up and check on it.

Vicky's family lived the closest to Deerhill, but they had not used the cottage in over two years, except when Doug, her father, came up to close it each winter. The summer before last Doug had been teaching in Germany, and last year they commuted between their apartment in New York City and a great-aunt's house outside Washington, D.C., while Vicky's mother researched her thesis at the Library of Congress. With her research done, Nan decided Deerhill would be a great place to write.

BIG DEAL, Vicky printed on the dust-covered desk. Washington may have been hot and muggy, but at least she had had her great-aunt Rae and together they'd had the Smithsonian. She could still see the display of gowns donated by former first ladies. Some day they would show her gown in there, too, not because she was a President's wife, but because she was *the* first lady, First Lady President. Aunt Rae said it could happen.

VICKI. VICKEE. VICKIE. VIKKI. VICTORIA, she traced. She'd have to decide which spelling before then.

Her brother stomped into the living room. Vicky quickly brushed the desk top clean. "Pick up all your garbage?"

"I want the guest house," said Skip.

"Guest house? You can't go back on your word. Besides, I'm not getting stuck with the attic, runt."

"You tricked me. You said the attic's better. I was just up there. It's hot!"

"Can I help it if you believed me? A deal's a deal."

2

"No way," her brother argued.

"No way what?" Nan dropped her suitcases and a sleeping bag in the doorway from the kitchen.

Vicky folded her arms high on her chest and smiled. "As usual, my baby brother is trying to get out of an agreement we made." Her mother shot her one of her "you-are-the-oldest-and-you-should-set-an-example" looks. Vicky didn't care, because she was right and being right excused a lot, including looking down her nose at Skip.

"You two work this out amicably or else I may take the guest house myself," Nan threatened. "A few lamps and it would make the perfect study."

"You never make him live up to his commitments." Vicky stalked past her mother.

"Hey — where are you going?" Skip called.

"To the guest house. Squatter's rights."

"No, you don't." Skip ran after her.

"Victoria Prentiss Seymour," she could hear her mother say.

Some summer this was going to be. All kid stuff, thought Vicky, as she turned an ankle, struggling to remain ahead of Skip on the path. Already, Nan couldn't think about anything but her history of women missionaries, and her father would be in New York most of the time. So here she was, in seventh grade — well, practically — stuck with a fifth-grader. Not even a fifth-grader yet, not until September.

To make things worse, Skip was stupid. By the time Vicky was in fourth grade, she was learning beginning algebra, she had read the entire Narnia series and both *Alice's Adventures in Wonderland* and *Through the Looking*

Glass, and she had borrowed every book on American history in the children's library.

Skip hadn't even started.

He was so far behind that Vicky had decided to take his education in hand. Whenever she could, she read to him about the Presidents, starting with Washington, and she showed him how to do the brain-teasers in a paperback she had bought at the Smithsonian, which was not easy because Skip hated school. (He had Mrs. Harper for fourth grade. Everybody who got Harp the Carp hated school for at least one year.)

Vicky pictured herself as a super-teacher, like Helen Keller's Annie Sullivan, piercing through Skip's ignorance to release his trapped brain. But nothing she did helped. Skip was still getting Satisfactories and Needs to Improve's on his report card, while Vicky had always gotten Outstandings, even from Harp the Carp.

Her mother would say Skip was average — people didn't have to be gifted for others to enjoy them — and she would list Skip's good qualities: a cheerful disposition, quick to forgive, and a lively sense of curiosity. It was always lively curiosity, as if plain curiosity were not enough.

In Vicky's circle of friends average was dumb. Everybody in her family was smart. All her friends were smart. Their families were smart. Everybody she knew was smart — except Skip.

By now Skip had caught up with her. She pretended to ignore him. It was very difficult to be the only one with a dumb brother. She wanted to correct him all the time, and worse, she felt ashamed she had not found a way to *make* Skip learn. She supposed she'd have to let him take the guest house. It was the price she paid for her failure.

4

Halfway to the pond a stand of pines shielded the guest house from the brilliant early June day. On the door to the green building hung a neatly painted sign that read: THE OUTHOUSE.

"That's new," said Vicky. Skip snickered.

He went inside. "Hey, four beds!" He bounced on the nearest cot.

In the dim light the cabin resembled a garage more than a sleeping place. A mattress and a broken chair rested against one wall. A hubcap hung on a row of coathooks. Vicky ran her finger over the dresser. Underneath the gray soot it was a distasteful mustard color.

"I'll take this one," said Skip, after trying each of the beds.

"You can have all of them. I'm not sleeping in this filth."

"Aww, Vick, we can clean. It's more fun with both of us. I don't want to stay down here all by myself."

"It's yours, little brother," Vicky said, leaving the cabin.

Careful of the tree roots and loose pebbles this time, she picked her way down the path for a glimpse of the pond. At the end of the service road that led to the beach, three boys on bicycles and a moped were fooling around in the small parking lot, attempting wheelies and reverse wheelies. The kid on the moped was falling a lot. Vicky scowled, then returned to the cottage. As she passed the guest house again, she steeled herself to ignore her brother's call, but none came.

Vicky stopped at their VW station wagon in the yard and leaned through the open window for a red-and-yellow bag. Togetherness with Skip was bad enough. Togetherness in a pig sty was impossible. She hefted the bag. At least she had her books.

She had just settled comfortably into a story about a girl with supernatural powers — the heroine was looking through her mother and seeing the past — when she heard Skip shouting from the path. She rolled on the lumpy daybed and tried to concentrate, but the voice insisted.

"Get the flashlight. Quick! There's something trapped in the guest house. I can hear it."

"It's an allosaurus escaped from the Museum of Natural History," Vicky called. She expected Skip to laugh or protest. "Is this some kind of joke?"

"No. I promise. Hurry."

Vicky took her time fishing Skip's flashlight from his suitcase. He could have gotten it himself. When she arrived at the cabin, Skip pulled her to the doorway.

A faint sound scratched the air.

"It's just a squirrel on the roof," Vicky pooh-poohed, "or a tree branch."

"No. Not up there. It's down. Maybe under the bed."

Skip was right. The tinny echo came from close to their feet. Then it stopped. Vicky turned on the flashlight and swept the floorboards.

"Over here." Skip sprawled on his stomach. He reached under a cot and pulled out a yellowing paperback and a basketball sneaker stuffed with a sock. Skip sneezed.

"Quiet. I hear it again," Vicky whispered. "I got it! It's coming from underneath the floor. It has to be the boat." The guest house rested on cinder blocks, leaving a space below the floor of the cabin where they stored the canoe.

Vicky and Skip nearly tripped over each other in their haste for the outside.

They tugged and yanked at the metal boat. The scratching grew louder.

When they managed to haul it out, Skip gasped. "Oh, Vick. They're beautiful." Someone — some *thing* — had strewn dried pine needles in the bottom of the canoe. Three kittens, soft gray-brown with contrasting bars and here and there a stray leopard spot, mewed and clawed. Skip bent to touch.

"Don't!!" Vicky shrieked. Skip froze where he was. "The mother might kill them, if she smells people on their fur."

"Not cats. They're not wild."

"Some are."

Skip picked up a twig and waved it. "I'm not touching. See?" He grinned. "Lookit. They don't know how to play yet."

"That's because they're too little," Vicky said scornfully. Skip's cheeks reddened. "Don't get any ideas about taking them home. You've killed enough smelly animals already. Like the garter snake?" Her brother did not answer. "You found him on that hike and he baked in the car. Nan said you couldn't bring anything home this time."

"Aww, shut up. I wasn't going to." He threw the stick aside.

Skip whirled suddenly. Vicky looked up. In the city they would have said it was trucks backfiring, or cherry bombs. Out here it sounded like gunshots.

2

❦❦❦

Up the hill, above the Seymours' summer house, Lynn Davis was watching from the porch as her grandmother bent over the aluminum cans scattered on either side of the stone fence. The ones that could be reused she balanced on the wall.

She had been firing at those cans on and off all afternoon. Her grandmother often disappeared for a round of target practice. It was her way of getting off by herself. But this long at it was unusual even for her.

Something at lunch must have annoyed her. They were tuned to the noon news on the radio. An eighty-two-year-old woman in Center Sandwich drove through a stop sign, the announcer chirped, and into a group of children. Now the national news: Senator So-and-So criticized the President's lack of progress in the arms-control talks. An ex-movie star was on her fifth divorce. Blah. Blah. Blah. Lynn had stopped listening.

Her meal half-eaten, her grandmother pushed in her chair and began shooting apart the cans. In all probability she would never explain why. After sixteen summers on the farm, one for each year of her life, Lynn was accustomed to Grammer's impatience with idle talk. It was a welcome change from her mother, who always explained herself — explained, repeated, and justified, until she was right by the mere weight of her words.

One by one the row of cans lurched from the wall like wounded birds. The last burst was aimed at the weather-vane on top of the barn. A pinging, then the metal rooster whirled madly on its one leg.

"Here, I'll take that," said Lynn. The old woman stood as erect as her humped shoulders allowed and handed over the rifle. The gun barrel was hot to the touch. Lynn placed it gingerly in the living room rack and locked it.

"Grammer?" Lynn said, stepping back outside. Grammer was shorthand for Grandmother Davis. Her grandmother tapped her chair, letting Lynn know she could get on with it. "You want some dinner? I heated up leftovers."

"Mmm-hm," she replied, not making a move.

A hint of dusk was starting to fall, first in the eastern hills. Lynn could hear the crickets scrape, then her grandmother's straw rocker creak. Scrape. Creak. Scrape. Creak.

Lynn sat on the porch swing and drew in the good air until she could feel it in her toes. It didn't matter that there weren't kids here her own age. She enjoyed the emptiness: No more choices. No more grinding to make an A on her world history exam. No more struggling to say no to riding in a car with kids she knew had been drinking. No more wanting, and fearing, to be like the other sophomore girls who settled for C's and never refused a ride. And no more hiding from her mother.

Grammer's illness had been lucky timing — for Lynn, anyway. As early as last January her mother had been pressuring her to apply for a summer job as a counselor at a day camp near their home in New Jersey. Somebody who was a friend of somebody else's could get her in. Lynn assumed she would have to.

For as long as she could remember, she could not stand next to her mother, who was petite, bustling with energy, and perfect in every detail, without feeling too something — too slow, too quiet, too slouched.

This last year was especially bad, with her father away on business for days at a time. Lynn couldn't do anything right — so she lied. About how hard the exam was, even which dress she liked. She hated the lies, but she hated still more that her mother knew, as she tried to steal the truth from her with a stream of innocent-seeming questions.

Then in March Grammer had fallen ill with pneumonia. She was slow recovering and she sent away all the housekeepers Lynn's mother hired. "I don't want busybodies poking in my dirt," she had barked over the phone. Lynn's father — Grammer was his mother — was no help. They were starting to talk about putting her into a nursing home. Temporarily, they said, until she was rested enough to be back on her feet.

The idea revolted Lynn. Once Grammer was in a home she might not come out. Her mother predicted this pneumonia was the beginning of more to come. They had even put their name on a number of waiting lists — "just in case."

That was when she volunteered to look after Grammer herself. She was amazed at how easy it had been. Her father thought it was terrific; he knew what was going on at home. Her mother called the school, Lynn crammed like

crazy, took her finals early, and flew to New Hampshire.
It hadn't been long before Grammer was pretty much her
old self, except that she tired more easily.

The farm was hardly a farm anymore — a lot of uncul-
tivated land was all. Not much exciting happened. But
Lynn had her horse. And Grammer, at least, didn't invade
her with questions.

She coughed a little, breaking the silence. "Grammer,"
she said, "I've decided I'm staying on the farm with you."

Grammer laughed a sly laugh. "I don't see there's reason to do any deciding about it. You're here and no place
else, the best I can make out."

"I mean I don't want to go back in the fall."

Grammer fell quiet. "I see."

"If it's okay with you."

"Okay with me isn't the matter, is it?" The rocker
creaked and paused. "Your mother agree to this?"

"No. Not yet," Lynn added, wishing.

"She puts a lot of importance on that fancy high school
of yours. Not like ours. Only learning, no extras here."

"I wouldn't mind."

"Is it to spite your mother? Doesn't take much to be
spiteful. Like yanking on a rope that goes between you
and the one you're spiting. No matter how far apart the
two ends are, a person's tied, till they can let go of the line.
Nothing free in spite."

"I don't know," said Lynn. Probably it was spite.

Scrape. Creak. Scrape. Creak. Then it was Grammer's
turn to interrupt their silence. "Some people have no business driving a car," she murmured.

Lynn puzzled, but she knew better than to ask. Grammer had a habit sometimes of considering matters out loud.

"Two youngsters injured, they said, and a little baby killed. Terrible waste. The Lord would have done better to take an old woman."

The accident in Center Sandwich. Details Lynn didn't know she had heard came floating back.

"Nobody's perfectly fine one minute and witless the next. There are signs," said Grammer, "but she was too foolish to admit to it. Lord. Lord. Have mercy. Spare us from the same conceit. Have mercy," she repeated, trailing off.

Her grandmother had been out there all afternoon, Lynn grasped suddenly, trying to determine if she showed these signs, whatever they were. Except there were no signs. Grammer's aim was absolutely steady. Darn her mother. She started it, creating an uproar over Grammer's needing help, when she would have recovered just as fast with canned soups and a dusty living room.

Grammer snorted. "Guess it's that time. Like the horseflies. The city people come buzzing again."

She was watching two figures, a boy and a girl, the girl the bigger of the two, trudging slowly up Deerhill Road. They seemed to be searching for something among the weeds at the side of the road. "Nosy critters, city people," said Grammer.

"I'm city," said Lynn.

"No real Davis is city."

"Suburban, then."

"Where you're born has no bearing on it," her grandmother shot back. "It has to do with knowing what you got to do and doing it, instead of crying in your milk. All's city people have is money where they ought to be back-bone."

Was she a real Davis? Most of the time Lynn didn't feel much like she had Grammer's kind of backbone.

The two children were approaching the house. "Hey, it's the Seymour kids," said Lynn. Nan must be here, too, she thought to herself.

"Who?" said Grammer, squinting.

"Don't you remember? I used to play with them down at the beach. They sure have changed." Lynn watched as they came up the drive. Three summers ago Vicky was a chubby blonde. She had grown a lot prettier. Now it was Skip who was the chubby one.

"Hi," said Vicky.

"Hi yourself," Lynn answered. "It's been a long time. Are you here for the summer?" They nodded. "Great. The last time I saw you, Skipper, you were missing a bunch of teeth. Guess you found some spare parts."

Skip flushed. "You look different, too." His eyes dropped to Lynn's feet.

Lynn grinned and showed her calluses. "I still can't stand shoes." She motioned toward Deerhill Road. "Did you lose something?"

"We're looking for a mother cat," said Vicky. "We found some kittens. We think maybe the mother is sick, or she might have been hit. She hasn't been back to take care of them."

"They're pretty little," said Skip.

"I haven't seen any. How about you, Grammer?"

Grammer's chair was going again. "Nope. Haven't seen any stranger cats, dead or alive. Lot of horseflies, though."

Vicky noticed the contempt in the old woman's reply.

She looked in the wrinkle-crusted face. Crabby old Mrs. Davis. She had almost forgotten. She tugged at Skip. "Let's go."

"Wait." He turned to Lynn. "Do you still have your horse?"

"Sure. But old Smoke's gotten lazy this winter. Like my grandmother here," she teased.

Grammer harumphed. "Having you under foot would make anybody lazy. Snatching away the dishes before I hardly dirtied them and digging up the carrots before they're full-grown so I won't get out there on my hands and knees. Why, it'd make anybody lazy. I say 'Shoo' and she laughs. See, there she goes."

Grammer leaned forward in her rocker, inspecting Vicky and Skip. "Now that I see you close, I can tell you aren't city people."

"But we are. We're from New York," Skip blurted.

"I mean the tourist kind. Lots of people here view tourist season as a blessing. They go waving their money around like they got some kind of new religion. Not me. I can do without tourist dollars, thank you." She focused on Skip. "You don't strike me as the money-waving type."

"No, ma'am," said Skip, stepping closer to his sister. "I only get a dollar-fifty a week for allowance."

Vicky wanted to tell him to never mind her — she was an old bully — when she heard her mother's voice behind them. "Is that Lynn Davis still throwing her shoes like a wild colt?"

In one leap Lynn's long legs bolted over the porch railing. Then she stopped short and stood before Nan, looking embarrassed. Nan took Lynn in her arms, surrounding her with a big hug.

14

Nan studied Lynn's lanky features and the short-cropped hair. Suddenly she groaned. "What on earth happened to your gorgeous long braids?"

Oh ick, thought Vicky. Nothing was worse than her mother fussing about growing up. What else were kids supposed to do?

"They're in a drawer at home. Once in a while I try them on." Lynn giggled.

Grammer hawked and spat in the background. Nan stepped to the porch, offering her hand. "How are you, Mrs. Davis?"

The old lady ignored the gesture. "About the same."

"Grammer had a hard winter with the flu and then pneumonia. I came up to help out," said Lynn. "She's getting her strength, though, aren't you, Grammer?"

"Good enough to give you trouble," she answered curtly. The rocker slid backward and Grammer went inside, followed by a rude bang.

"I forget how cool the evenings are here. And we don't have sweaters," Nan said. "We should be going, too."

For once Vicky was grateful her mother always knew the right thing to say. Who could chitchat after that?

Skip called to Lynn from the road, "You can come see the kittens if you want to."

"Great. Maybe tomorrow."

Beneath the trees the road was so dark that until Vicky's sandals touched bottom it felt like trying to walk on water.

"I remember you were scared to get on her horse," Skip taunted.

"How could you remember that? You're too dumb to remember anything."

Nan dropped into step alongside. "Easy, you two."

"How come she wouldn't shake hands?" Vicky asked.

"Mrs. Davis?" Her mother chuckled. "She still hasn't forgiven my family for buying her property."

"What property? You mean the cottage? She owned it?"

"We rented it from her when I was a girl. Then times were harder, and Mrs. Davis had to sell or go under. Your grandfather didn't want to see her lose the farm, so he offered her top dollar. But he could be as stubborn as she was. He wouldn't buy without access to the pond. It took an entire season to close the deal, and afterward Mrs. Davis never spoke to your grandfather again, and she was barely civil to the rest of us."

"But he did her a favor —"

Nan's arm slipped around Vicky's waist. "That was precisely the problem."

"Where's Mr. Davis?"

"Her husband died years ago. I never met him." Nan paused, as if to decide how to say what was on her mind. "When you've been such a loner — well, it must be especially difficult to grow old, and dependent."

"I don't feel sorry for her. I feel sorry for Lynn." Her mother did not answer. She just pulled Vicky close.

Lynn swallowed more of the soothing night air, as she watched Nan and her children disappear down the road. Those boys were hot-rodding on the beach again. She could hear the moped.

The living room appeared empty. "Did you go to bed already?" Lynn groped for the light switch behind the door.

"Grammer!" She saw her grandmother slumped in the

far corner over the back of an armchair, struggling to right herself.

"Turn it off, child," her grandmother begged.

Lynn ran to her. "Why didn't you call me? Here, sit. We'll put your feet up. Should I call the doctor?" Lynn's heart rushed frantically.

Grammer closed her eyes, her head sinking backward. A circle of white ringed her mouth. Perspiration beaded the downy furrows above her lips.

"Grammer?"

Her hand floated in a kind of hello, then fell. "I'm all right," she whispered. "A glass of cold water will fix me fine."

Lynn returned with the water quickly. Grammer was mopping her forehead. When she saw Lynn, she managed a smile. "Don't scowl so. A little dizzy, child, is all." Her voice wheezed, caught on something in her throat. The glass trembled as she sipped. "If I don't look foolish. It's my medicine. I swear it makes me worse. Forget to take it one day and I topple over neater than a tree hit by lightning. Last time I woke up in my garden." She laughed weakly.

"Last time?"

"Must of given the crows something to cackle over for days. Ever notice how they talk? Like decaying old ladies in the back pew. The back pew surely cured me of church-going."

"Grammer — what medicine?" Lynn demanded. "I didn't know you took any except your vitamins."

"Who wants to bore a young girl with pills?"

"How can I take care of you, if I don't know you're supposed to be taking medicine? What are the pills for?"

17

Grammer's lips sealed in a line. "I'm calling the doctor," said Lynn.

"Put one finger on the phone and I can tell you you're no longer welcome here, child. Don't look at me like that. I couldn't mean what I say more. If baby-tending is what you're here for, you can pack up and go back to New Jersey. Plenty of rice pudding needed there."

Grammer smoothed the wrinkles in the lap of her cotton dress and continued to talk as if nothing out of the ordinary had occurred. "Sit down, child," she bossed. "And quit staring."

Lynn could not believe it. She'd known her grandmother all her life. Who was this person?

3

❧❧❧

Tucking her bare feet under herself, Lynn huddled over a steamy cup of hot chocolate. The mug felt good on her stiff fingers.

"Icicles in the air this morning, child. That sweatshirt enough out here on the porch?"

"Grammer. I didn't realize you were up. How are you feeling?" Lynn ventured cautiously.

Grammer gave her a look that told Lynn she should not have asked. "I can't stand people whimpering. Nothing worse than calling out the doctor when you don't have something worth rousing him for." Then Grammer fixed her gaze on a clump of white cedars on the far side of the pond and swallowed. "You know you're the only one in this stuck-up family, outside of me, that cares to be here, don't you?"

"Daddy likes the farm."

"Oh, for a vacation maybe, but not to call it home. He cares about his white shirts and his clean fingernails too much."

"Do you — did you take it yet?" said Lynn.

"There's no need to remind me." Grammer managed a small chuckle. "Dear, dear me. Time was, if I held my teeth together tight and put one foot in front of the other, I could make my way through anything. All it takes is starch, I said. Lord knows, I had to do it often enough. Now it's pills holding me together." She lapsed into herself.

The feeling that in some way her grandmother was a stranger flitted over Lynn again. Grammer seldom talked about the Davis family history, but every once in a while her father would drink a few too many and repeat it word for word — how Grammer did not bear him until she was nearly forty and how she was widowed soon after, how they had scrabbled to make a meager existence. Lynn's mother complained Grammer would have lived poor, no matter how well off she was. Didn't her father sell the land across the pond for her at a handsome price and invest it well? — very well, her mother would add — and still she insisted on holing up like a pauper on the farm.

But what else did Grammer grit her teeth to get through? Lynn wished she could ask. Instead, she put down her cocoa and held her grandmother's arm.

Grammer patted her hand, then released herself. "It's good you're here," she said.

Vicky munched on her breakfast cereal as noisily as she could. Her mother and Lynn sat across the table from each other, chatting about summers past — when Vicky and Skip were *in*fants — which annoyed Vicky no end. Lynn couldn't be that much older — three and a half years at most. Oh, all right, four years. Besides, she wasn't Nan's guest. Lynn came to see the kittens. That made her their guest.

Tap. Tap. Rat-ta-ta-tap tap TAP! Vicky's spoon danced on the sugar bowl.

"Victoria, that bothers me," her mother said, and she continued her conversation, looking not at all bothered.

Vicky let her breakfast dishes clatter into the sink. She found Skip on the attic stairs absorbed in a super-heroes comic. "Okay, let's go see the cats," Vicky ordered.

"What about Lynn?"

Vicky shrugged. "That's her tough luck."

Skip required no further encouragement. He was off and running. When they neared the guest house, Skip pranced ahead on tiptoes, then fell to his knees and crawled in circles, sniffing the air and examining broken weed stalks.

"What are you supposed to be? Doggy D.A.?" It was a good thing no one could see him, thought Vicky.

"I'm looking for animal signs — to see if the mother cat's been here. I read about them in a magazine once."

"The only signs you can read are on a post. Quit fooling around and help pull out the canoe."

20

"Hey, what's this?" Skip dragged a makeshift box from beneath a sumac that overhung the path. Withered vines and leafy branches had been woven through the slats, forming a crude camouflage. Skip looked into the opening. "Phew. It stinks."

"Throw that thing away. It's a piece of junk."

He tipped the box on end and followed his sister. "I bet it's a trap."

"For what? To catch overweight mice? It's on our property. Nobody can put traps on our property without our permission." By then they had reached the guest house. It was awkward to stoop and pull at the same time. Vicky and Skip yanked unevenly.

"I don't hear any scratching," said Skip.

A beam of light through the trees glanced off the aluminum boat with blinding intensity. It took a few moments before they could make out what they were looking for.

"Oh-h-h no," Skip groaned. There in his bed of pine needles a kitten lay motionless, a tiny bud of a tongue hanging from his mouth.

Tears welled in Skip's eyes. Gently he nudged the other two kittens. One mewed faintly. "This one's alive," he said, as the tears spilled.

Skip tore up the hill, screaming for Nan.

Vicky knelt next to the canoe and ran a finger over the dead kitten. The fur was like wispy dandelion fluff. When she pinched a bit of its coat, the fur tuft fell out easily. The remaining kittens nuzzled at it, rooting for a teat. Vicky wanted to pull them away, but she was afraid to touch. If one stopped breathing in her hands, she didn't know what she would do.

21

Soon her mother and Lynn were coming down the path. "Poor baby," Nan whispered, when she saw the dead kitten.

Almost before she realized what she was doing, Vicky flung a wild, careless arm at her mother. Nan looked stunned, then grabbed Vicky's wrist. "It's all your fault," Vicky shouted. "If you hadn't made us wait — You killed it!" The thrashing ended, and Vicky dissolved into tears.

Lynn watched, absorbed, as Nan soothed her and let her cry. Vicky didn't know how lucky she was. Lynn scooped the kittens out of the canoe and sheltered them in the crook of her elbow. "They're pretty weak," she said to Nan.

"Come on, Vick," Nan urged, "we'll do better by these two."

In the kitchen Vicky stood aside, weepy yet, while Lynn and her mother prepared a place for the kittens. They transferred them to a small carton they lined with shredded papers and a blanket. "Wouldn't you know it," said Nan. She was rummaging through cupboard drawers and the medicine cabinet. "No eyedroppers. Anywhere."

"How about a spoon?" Lynn suggested.

"Spoon's too big." Nan snapped her fingers. "I've got it. Vick, in with the games and things in the attic, see if there are any toy baby bottles."

Pawing through the dusty boxes, Vicky started to feel a little better. One box was brimful with Halloween costumes and dress-up clothes saved for rainy days. Another held at least a couple of dozen green midget teapots, but there were no baby bottles to be had. She went downstairs. "Nope."

"Ouch," said Nan.

"What about sponges? You could break off a piece of a new one and squeeze the milk into their mouths." Vicky was careful to say *you*. No way was she taking responsibility for those kittens, living or dying.

"Ex!" said Lynn.

Nan squinted. "Ex?"

Vicky and Lynn exchanged glances. "Ex is for excellent," said Lynn. "You know. Like deece for decent?"

"Ohh, now I gotcha." Nan winked. "Gotcha is old-fashioned for understand."

Both girls rolled their eyes and signaled thumbs down in unison.

Right about then they heard Skip's bicycle dropping in the yard. No one had noticed he was gone. He came in, clutching a battered paper sack. "Cripes, I thought you were down at the guest house, so I went there first." He held up the bag. "Here's the milk."

"Were we out?" said Nan.

"Vicky and I finished it this morning. Remember you didn't have any for your coffee?"

"I do now." Nan put her arm about Skip and playfully cuffed his head. "What a quick-thinking kid I've got. Right, Vicky?"

Skip was beaming. Sometimes he really did surprise her.

Nan sterilized a sponge, and Lynn and Skip set to work. They hovered over the kittens the rest of the morning, switching roles as nursemaids and observers, but the animals could not seem to grasp what was expected of them. In time their coats were soaked and matted.

Skip dribbled more milk onto the lips of the kitten cradled in his lap, trying to coax it to open its mouth. "He's given up. I know it."

23

"They're only tired from all this handling, Skipper," said Lynn, but she feared he was right, that the kittens were so weak they had lost their sucking reflex. According to her father, that happened to baby animals sometimes. Grammer was the one neighbors used to call on to birth a calf or tend a sick pig, and he tagged along, and when that happened, when they couldn't suckle anymore, he wouldn't want to see the rest.

Lynn helped Skip dry the kittens as best they could and return them to the carton where they lay in limp heaps. They were so small their claws looked like fingernail clippings. How much did something that tiny need to eat in order to survive?

"Don't stop now," said Vicky.

"Oh yeah? You got any more good ideas, like sponges? Why don't you try feeding them, if you're so smart?" her brother retorted.

"I think it's time we drove into Meredith for eyedroppers," said Nan, heading off an argument.

"Let me try my grandmother first. It's closer," Lynn suggested. "She's not big on medicines, but she never throws anything away."

"Great."

Skip hooted at Vicky and ran out the door behind Lynn. "Wait for me. I want to ride on your horse."

"Why don't you go, too?" Nan prodded. Vicky shook her head no. She was already feeling anxious about the kittens; she wasn't interested in scaring herself more by riding on a horse. "It was a good idea," said Nan, after they had gone.

"An idea isn't good until it works," said Vicky.

"You shouldn't be so hard on yourself, Vick." Vicky

would not answer. "Well, leaving the kittens alone certainly wasn't ex," sighed Nan. "I thought it was the right thing. Humans are always so ready to impose themselves on other life. We destroy animals if they are injured, tame them if they are wild, skin them or stuff them if they are beautiful.

"When you were little, there was a deer that used to come to the pond. One leg had shortened up. Probably it was an old injury. Whatever it was, the deer had healed itself. I was always impressed by that. Maybe putting it out of its misery would not have been a kindness — I didn't want to interfere, Vick. The mother was the best one to care for them."

Vicky smiled. "Don't be so hard on yourself, Mom."

4

❦❦❦

Grammer was at work in the potting shed where Lynn had left her hours before. Breathlessly, Skip explained their errand.

"I got 'em. Even have two," Grammer replied, inverting a clay pot and tapping out the plant. She examined the root ball, then looked up and said, "But I don't know that I ought to let you have them."

"You've gotta be kidding," said Lynn.

"I most certainly am not," Grammer said sharply.

"They're not eating," Skip protested.

"Young man, I don't waste sympathy on animals that had no business being born. Out on a farm or in the woods, you let what's supposed to die, die. You can't be throwing away time and tears on useless critters. That goes for people as well as animals." She crammed the plant into its pot.

"Oh fer — Jiminy Christmas. Take the blamed things. They're in my drawer with the kitchen tools. Seems to me I used them to oil something. You'll have to clean them," she warned.

But Skip's expectant gaze did not waver. "Well?" she challenged. "Now what does he want?" the old woman sputtered.

"You could save them," said Skip, "if you felt like it. You know a lot about animals. Coming over, Lynn said so."

"Daddy told me you used to get calls from people miles away to help with sick animals," said Lynn.

"That was business. I needed farmhands and I paid for it with doctoring." Grammer paused, wiping her hands on her apron. "Oh, all right. But I promise you, if they're too far gone, I'll drown the kits before I pick up a hand to nurse them."

"Ya-a-a-a-ay!" Skip screeched, throwing his fists in a show of victory.

Grammer's face flushed. "I gave up this nonsense when your father grew enough to do a day's work."

It took all Skip's persuasive powers to convince Grammer that the kittens should not be moved. "Haven't been down there in years," she grumbled. "Don't know why I should start now." Then she refused to drive. "A waste of gas to go such a puny way. Lord, I walked that road more times than you can count."

Lynn, remembering the night before, was not about to let her walk. "What if you fell and broke a hip?" That was what her mother seemed to dwell on since Grammer's illness, certain it would be the next catastrophe. Lynn was surprised to hear herself repeating it, since it always annoyed her.

"Yes. Yes. I could crumble — like that. What do you propose to do, child — haul me in a little red wagon? It's walk or nothing."

At long last they reached a compromise, and Lynn and Skip helped Grammer onto Smoke. She rode alone, side-saddle, carrying a can of Karo corn syrup under her arm, and looking, Lynn thought, as imposing as any Queen of England.

When Lynn's grandmother entered, Nan was all flutter and nervous laughter. Vicky had seldom seen her mother so giddy. "Much of the house is exactly as you had it," said Nan.

Mrs. Davis thumped her tin on the kitchen counter and went straight to inspect the kittens. "I don't need to drown them," she chuckled. "You're doing it already."

Then she held up a kitten for what seemed to Vicky an unnecessarily long time. The chuckle decayed into a frown.

"What do you think?" said Skip, concerned.

She studied Skip. "No way you could know, I suppose."

Skip shot a confused look at his sister. Vicky shrugged. Then they looked to Lynn, who returned a blank look.

"My, you are a sorry one," Mrs. Davis murmured to

the kitten. "Their eyes are open. I'd say they're a good two or three weeks old. More, possibly." She hesitated. "Okay, warm the milk."

"Ya-a-ay!" Skip shouted again.

"Hold on, young man. You want to let me know you're appreciative — you do it" — Mrs. Davis whispered — "quietly. I'm too old for my ears to enjoy hollering. Agreed?" Skip clamped his mouth shut and nodded violently. "I'm glad we're understood."

Thin, amber drips streaked the label and sides of the syrup can. Mrs. Davis poured a little into a pan of milk. "One time we had a cow die, giving birth. The calf lived," she said, tamping down the lid, "and I went to put her on another cow, but she was drying up and the calf wasn't taking to her. Your daddy, Lynn, thought maybe the cow didn't taste good. We fixed that. Rubbed Karo on her udder. Used Karo ever since," she said with a laugh.

After Lynn's grandmother tested the milk and filled an eyedropper, she pointed to Vicky. "Come here, and I'll show you how to do it."

"But I can't," Vicky stammered. Mrs. Davis humphed and waited. Vicky stepped forward.

Mrs. Davis slipped a little finger into the kitten's mouth to hold it open, while she inserted the tip of the dropper and squeezed with the other fingers. The kitten winced, its tongue thrusting feebly at the dropper. "Simple, eh? Now you try it." She handed Vicky the dropper first, then the kitten.

The warm tongue worked against Vicky's fingertip. She could feel tiny points inside, maybe teeth.

"Go on."

28

She squeezed a few timid drops, only to have the liquid dribble out when the little mouth closed.

"Tip the head back a bit. Won't hurt him."

Skip, meanwhile, had plunged ahead with the other kitten. "Look, it's eating!" he announced gleefully, refilling his eyedropper.

"Don't give up, Vick," her mother prodded.

"What if I jab my finger in too far?" complained Vicky, but she tried again. Gradually her nervousness faded and more of the food disappeared along its intended path. Press the bulb, then wait while the kitten did his part, squirt again. She did it — she could feed the kitten! "Hey, Mrs. Davis," Vicky called, "we'll have a Karo milk shake to go."

"They've had enough now. Let them rest." Lynn's grandmother stepped closer to look at the kitten. "Greedy little varmints," she said, startling Vicky with her anger.

Lynn could see her grandmother had been tiring, leaning into the table to steady herself or holding on to the stove top. She jumped quickly from her seat on the counter and suggested they head home.

They were leaving, when Grammer halted as if reminded of something. "Mind you," she spoke crossly, "I shouldn't have lifted a finger for those kits. Unless I miss my guess, they'll prove to be a burden to you yet."

"What did she mean?" asked Skip, after the door closed.

Nan shook her head. "Probably nothing. She was tired. You know how grumpy you get," she said, tousling Skip's hair. Skip ducked out of reach. His face was intent, trying to understand.

29

When Nan turned away, Vicky drew large circles in the air around her right ear for Skip. The puzzled look remained; that did not answer his question either.

Later that evening Vicky, Skip, and Nan held a pow-wow to discuss feedings. They settled on every hour and a half, since Nan said it was not unusual to feed a newborn infant every couple of hours and the kittens' tummies were much smaller. That way Skip and Vicky each could have a three-hour stretch to sleep between feedings. The children experimented with milk and the syrup that Mrs. Davis left behind until they mixed a batch that tasted like her sweet milk. Nan was going to give the kittens their ten-thirty feeding so Skip and Vicky could go to bed early, and she would set the alarm for Skip to take the first shift.

No matter how she lay in bed Vicky could not find a comfortable position. She hoped Nan wouldn't trick them and take extra feedings. The kittens were hers now. She had fed them. It was her responsibility to take care of them. Then she remembered the dead kitten.

"Skip," she whispered, "that kitten's in the canoe." He stirred, and rolled over.

Quietly, Vicky tiptoed downstairs. Her mother was poring over her note cards. She passed unnoticed through to the kitchen, down the enclosed walkway connecting the house and the barn. There she found a shovel and the flashlight and carried them to the guest house. In the shadows behind the building she dug a shallow grave and laid the body inside. She smoothed over the grave and carefully marked it with a stick. Skip might want to know where it was.

On her way through the kitchen again Vicky stopped at

30

the kittens' box. Their rib cages swelled just enough to reassure her they were alive. These would be the best cared-for kittens ever, she resolved. When she put her mind to something, she always did it well, that is, except for educating Skip, and she had not given up on him — not yet.

By the time she climbed into bed, Vicky was chilled. She yawned — the squirmy feeling had gone — and rolled into a ball under the covers. Tomorrow she would start her brother on negative numbers.

5

❦❦❦

A day and a half of heavy rainfall had eroded the old logging trail. In several places the soil was washed down to the tree roots, creating a drop-off around which Lynn and her horse had to pick their way carefully to avoid sliding in the mud.

Deerhill Road would have been safer, but after her daily visit at the Seymours', habit sent Lynn down the wide trail and through the trees on the point across the shortcut, which connected the logging trail with their beach path.

In the few weeks since they arrived, Vicky and Skip had adopted her like an older sister: They sought out her opinion and involved her in their squabbles. Lynn in turn was helping them learn to ride.

Occasionally she was aware that Vicky and Skip were

too young for her. She felt it keenly the night they rolled up in sleeping bags on the beach (complete with alarm clock to feed the kittens). Skip's nervousness reminded her too much of Girl Scout sleepovers. But most of the time the age difference didn't matter. Being an only child, Lynn thought, it was nice to have a borrowed brother and sister.

Lynn eased Smoke onto the shortcut and relaxed a bit; the footing was better here. She shifted the fresh tin of Karo she carried to the other arm. She had noticed last time that the old container was running low. Grammer stored cartons of the stuff in her food cellar. She wouldn't mind.

The Karo was an excuse, really. Vicky and Skip's father was driving up from New York for an extended Fourth of July weekend. It was midafternoon. He might already be there, she thought, her stomach churning. She hoped he would not spoil things.

Suddenly something spewed a string of metallic hacks and burps, then a single loud outburst. That moped again! Smoke bolted from the shortcut, lashing Lynn through an unfriendly curtain of branches. Finally she reined him in and they stood at a safe distance.

It was a worn silver Puch with mag wheels. The boy pedaled furiously trying to start up again. What was he doing out here anyway? This was no place for his bike, not after the kind of wet weather they were having. Lynn knew a little about mopeds. When she turned sixteen she had angled for one, but her mother was so worked up about motorcycle accidents that Lynn abandoned the idea.

She retrieved the fallen can of syrup and backtracked to where the moped was mired. Water had collected in a shallow depression below the path, turning it into a mud hole.

The boy stopped pedaling and turned the switch on the fuel valve. His jeans were mud-spattered and his face crimson and sweaty. "Hey, I'm sorry," he said. "I didn't mean to scare your horse. Honest. I didn't see you," and he looked forlornly at the bike.

"Forget it," said Lynn. She pressed her knees and Smoke started forward.

"Hey," the boy called. Lynn stopped. "You think you could give me a lift?"

"A lift? Where?"

The boy's face reddened more. "Down to the highway. I can hitchhike from there to my brother's house. I gotta come back in the pickup for this thing." He cursed under his breath and climbed off the bike, kicking at it — missing deliberately.

"How did you do that, anyway?"

"I was trying to jump the hole."

"You didn't make it."

"Yeah." He clearly did not think it was a joking matter. He pushed the moped off the kickstand and rolled it to a tree, where he locked and chained the bike.

"You going to leave it there?"

"Better here than down by the pond. Peds don't have keys like cars. Anybody could take it. No one uses this bike unless I say so." He wiped his hands on the front of his T-shirt. "You live around here?"

"Well, I stay on my grandmother's farm."

"I knew I'd seen your horse before." Lynn assumed he meant on the beach. "So I'm Howie," he said, abruptly changing the subject. "Do I get that ride?"

Lynn didn't know how to refuse without feeling like a snob. "Why not." She waited while he tucked his bungee

33

cords in a pocket and unstrapped his black helmet, slipping it over his arm. She reached down and helped him aboard.

"Do you have to have a license to drive a moped here?" Lynn asked once they were moving. "We do in New Jersey."

"Well, you're supposed to," Howie answered from behind her shoulder. "Except I don't have one."

"How come?"

"You have to be sixteen to get a license. I won't be sixteen until October. My mother and father don't even know I have a bike. I keep it at my brother's house."

"You could get into a lot of trouble."

"I don't ride where the cops are. Mostly I ride at my brother's place — that's legal — and down at the pond."

"It's not so long. Why don't you wait until your birthday?"

"You crazy?" Howie laughed. "You take that Puch away from me — man, I'm dead. Really ticks me off I can't be on the gas right now. I'll have to wait until my brother can help me fix it if I've got dirt in my carb. Summer's his busy time. He rebuilds motorboat engines at the marina over on Winnipesaukee. Besides, the cops only hassle the kids that hang out at the Dairy Palace. I stay away from there."

They rode in silence for a while. Lynn directed her horse along the beach to the access road, then to Deerhill Road. Fortunately, they would be at the highway in a few minutes.

Howie probably was nice enough, but she knew the type. They didn't play sports, and they didn't have a lot of friends. All they had were their bikes, and they talked and breathed gasoline fumes from the time they got up until after dark. And whenever they were off their bikes, they paced. At least he had the sense to get a helmet. It gleamed with a brand-new shine. "I like the color," she said, motioning.

"Yeah? I made a deal with my brother. He wouldn't tell my mom about the bike, if I promised to wear it. He bought it for me. My dad wouldn't mind about the bike. It's my mom. Man, this stinks. I hope it's water in the sparkplug cap. I can dry that out."

"How?"

"With a hairdryer. I'll use my brother's girlfriend's." Lynn laughed. "No kidding. Lotta things I can fix myself — like my throttle cable broke one day. But a carb — you have to make all these adjustments and you need tools, you know?"

They had reached the highway. There were few cars. Lynn wondered how long a walk it was to Howie's brother's.

Howie slipped to the ground. "See ya around." He waved, walking backward.

She probably would — see him around. "Good luck with your bike."

Vicky woke, as cranky as when Nan kissed her and Skip and tucked them into bed for an afternoon nap. Vicky's throat was dry; her eyes itched. The attic was just too hot during the day for sleeping. Why did she let her mother talk her into a nap? Things weren't bad enough — she was worn out from getting up nights to feed the kittens — but Nan had to nag her about it, too.

She tried to slip off her cot. First the springs twanged.

Then she stubbed a toe and dropped her shoe. Oh phooey. What did she care if she woke Skip? Serve him right for being such a dismal student yesterday and *refusing* to listen when she explained the differences between *there, their,* and *they're*. All he did was smack his gum and make faces.

Downstairs, Vicky cast an angry, sidelong look at her mother as she marched for the kittens' box. Nan's staccato typewriter paused.

The kittens were dozing in a huddle. Vicky rattled a pan out of a lower cupboard, banging the pot beside it, and went to prepare the sweetened milk.

"Mother!" Vicky wailed. "The syrup's all gone." Big, loose tears tumbled over her cheeks.

Nan rose from the table. "Vick, you're exhausted. How about I feed them tonight?"

"No," Vicky sniffed. "You want to make them go too long between feedings. Besides, they're my responsibility."

"They don't need hand-feeding anymore. They could use a dish."

An unfamiliar horn tooted in the yard. Nan peered outside, still delivering her lecture. "I'm pleased you and Skip are taking this thing seriously, but there is a limit — " Nan stopped midsentence. "He's here!" she exclaimed. "It's your father!"

Sidling out from a foreign-made compact, his long frame unfolded like an accordion. Doug waved two small boxes just beyond Nan's reach. They were the typewriter ribbons she had asked him to bring when he came for the weekend. "What'll you give me for these?" he teased, kissing his wife. "They do have stores here, you know."

"But everything costs so much during tourist season."

"Ah ha! You admit it. You're a tourist. If you were a local, you'd know where to shop." Doug stooped to hug Vicky. "Hi ya, pal. I'm gonna skunk you at cribbage tonight." Vicky laughed, forgetting her crabbiness.

"Since the kids found the kittens I feel more like a hermit than a tourist," Nan answered. "They hover over them constantly, and they aren't getting any sleep."

Uh-oh, thought Vicky. If her father took Nan's side, it was all over. Just then Skip burst through the door. "Dad! What kind of car did you rent?" Doug was not the only one glad to see him.

For the next half hour Vicky and Skip courted their father with a stream of anecdotes about the kittens. "See how they wiggle when we pick them up? And when they push their noses at us like this, they're looking for milk," said Vicky.

Occasionally some detail would pique Doug's curiosity. "Look at this. They've got extra tufts on their ears. Mama Cat mixed it up with a porcupine," he said with a guffaw. But Vicky knew they were lost when he conducted a mock veterinary examination — on the cats first, then with them — prying open their mouths, their eyes, pretending to search their hair for fleas. Doug hated to give bad news straight.

"Okay, gang, good work," he said. "The kittens look fat and sassy. But what's your mother been doing? Locking you in the cellar? You're gray. You can turn gray in New York. I farmed you out here to put sunshine in those bones. You kids are going to start having fun."

"We are."

37

"Exercise. Picnics. Sleep. Good stuff like that. How about the cog railway tomorrow? We never made it last time."

Skip groaned. "That's a whole day, isn't it? We can't leave them that long."

"We'll take them with us."

"Remember the snake?" Vicky countered quickly. "They'll suffocate in the car." Her mother and father prided themselves on being fair-minded, always ready to hear out an opposing point of view, and Vicky knew how to use it to her advantage. The discussion soon stalemated.

What she had not counted on was her father's willingness to sacrifice his principles. He scratched his head, then folded his arms and tried to swagger. It would have been comic, except Vicky knew he was serious. "I am going to exercise my prerogatives as a parent," he announced. "Ahem. Mom and I are the wet-nurses tonight, and tomorrow we do two things. We rig a system so the cats can feed themselves. Number Two, we — "

"They'll drown!"

"I am not finished, Victoria," her father admonished. "I promise a safe, foolproof system. And Number Two. No more arguments. Clear? It's the cog railway or bust." Skip slumped visibly. Tie score, man on third, bottom of the ninth, and the ump called the game.

"Hi," a voice called hesitantly from the open doorway. "I saw you were nearly out of syrup. Grammer has plenty — "

"Lynn!" Skip whooped. "You can feed them!"

"She can *not*. She's coming with us," said Nan, and the outcry started anew.

Lynn stood offering the tin of syrup, waiting for the

commotion to die down. Doug took it from her. "Welcome to the monkey house," he said grinning. Lynn grinned back — things would not change, after all.

6

❧❧❧

Grammer was friendly the next morning, but that was not enough to reassure Vicky, who stiffly presented the box. Lynn felt a little sorry for her, particularly since she was the one who suggested they leave the kittens with Grammer. Nan and Doug had jumped at the idea. Once people got used to Grammer they realized she only pretended to be crabbed and mean.

The kitten in Grammer's palm purred as she stroked its chin. "This one's got a regular outboard motor on him. What do you call him?"

"We haven't named them yet," Skip answered. "Vicky doesn't want to."

Grammer lifted the cat's tail. "Yep. A he. You can bet on it. I'd call him Evinrude. This other one looks like a she. Haven't got any girl names right off. Maybe Cleo. She seems a bit of a Cleo to me."

When they started out for Mt. Washington, everybody in the car was quiet. The station wagon rolled past old farmhouses, many no longer part of working farms. In front of some there were vegetable and fruit stands built of graying scrap wood, often with just a tin can and a sign reminding customers to pay. Skip whistled. "Boy, they couldn't do that in New York." Here and there they saw entrances for campsites or maple sugar farms. Usually it was a dirt road that jutted off into the trees. A speeding car would have missed them easily.

After a sharp curve in the road, they came upon an aging two-story house that had been converted into a craft shop. Bulky wood trains, cars, and zoo animals paraded across the windows. A young man sat on a bench sanding a rhinoceros. He blew sawdust from its horn and held it up to the daylight. Skip hallooed out the window. The man waved.

"I've been thinking," Skip ventured after he pulled his head inside.

"Hooray," said Vicky.

Skip stuck his tongue out at her and went on talking. "I like the names Mrs. Davis gave the cats. I think we ought to keep them."

"Unh-uh. It's bad luck. Not until we're sure they're okay," said Vicky.

"Grammer thinks they look great," said Lynn.

"And you told me smart people aren't superstitious," Skip taunted.

Rapid-fire fashion, Doug called from the front, "All-those-in-favor-of-Evinrude-and-Cleo-signify-by-raising-the-hand-on-the-right-and-shouting-aye. Aye!"

"Aye."

"Aye."

"Do I get a vote?" Lynn asked.

"Of course."

"Then aye."

"Ratfink." Vicky pouted, sliding so low in the car seat her chin was resting on her shirt.

"Knock. Knock," called Doug.

Everyone except Vicky replied, "Who's there?"

After a few tired Knock-Knock's, Doug started them on camp songs. He looked silly with his arm dipping and sliding as if he were conducting, but Lynn enjoyed his clowning. "On Saturdays he listens to the opera and waves his baton at the radio the whole afternoon," Skip confided. Nan ordered Doug to pull over, so she could drive.

"What is a cow's favorite sound?" Doug yelled. No one answered. "Moo-sic!"

Skip faked a groan.

"Oh, I get it," said Lynn.

"No, don't," Vicky begged. "I can't stand a whole day of cow jokes."

"We've learned if you don't answer, Lynn," Nan said, laughing, "they go away."

Then Doug pretended to throw something at Vicky. "Take that, O daughter, doubter of cow jokes. And that!"

Vicky hurled it back, and soon the station wagon was full of invisible missiles and mock agony.

Nan stopped the car. "Come on, you guys, or we'll never get there." No one listened, and it was everyone for himself. At last the fun subsided except for an occasional giggle, bubbling to the surface.

They were rolling again, up and down crayon-green mountains, around sparkling lakes, along the main streets of clapboard villages, farther and farther from greedy kittens and sleepless nights. Vicky stretched her arms and legs in the drowsy sun. She did feel good.

The car's rhythm had nearly lulled her to sleep, when it swerved to the right, jerking her to wakefulness.

"It's the Peterson!" Nan cried. "My birthday place." In a meadow valley that seemed to stretch for miles, a wizened summer hotel stood alone. Two long arms reached from the main body, making it look for all the world like an old woman bent close to the earth, scooping up the tall grasses.

Every August, Nan explained, she was brought to the Peterson for her birthday. "We came for dinner. I wore my white embroidered gloves. You don't even own a pair, Vick. I used to think it was so-o proper to have individual pats of butter instead of a common butter dish. After dinner we'd sit on the verandah — "

"The *what?*"

"Porch." "The porch," Vicky and Lynn answered simultaneously.

"Poor Skipper," Doug commiserated, "now you've got two defenders of the King's English after your tongue."

Nan was oblivious. " — and we'd talk very, very quietly. When you children were small the hotel went out of business and they auctioned off all the contents. People bought bed linens and towels by the dozens. For pennies. Mother and I made one last visit. We bid on a box of green teapots — little ceramic pots, big enough to serve one person. They were cracked or the lids were missing, but we were the guardians of history that day."

So that's what those things were doing in the attic, thought Vicky.

Doug suggested they eat lunch there. Sprawled in the

42

grass, they picnicked on fruit and sandwiches, then Lynn and Vicky and Skip tramped around the hotel, peering in the windows and trying the many doors, with the echo of their footsteps for reply. Nan seemed satisfied, and they drove the rapid, twisting climb from the Peterson to Mt. Washington and the cog railway.

Quickly enough, a hot, smoky engine squealed beside them. From the cab the grimy-faced engineer flashed a pink smile, welcoming them aboard. As soon as they entered the narrow coach, they were enveloped in sound. One little boy covered his ears. His mouth opened wide, but the scream was swallowed in the roar from the engine and the wheels.

Notch by notch, the cogs bit into the center rail, pulling them skyward. As they slowly passed a group of hikers, people on the train waved or they snapped pictures. Lynn glanced at her lap. Her khakis were so heavily dotted with flecks of ash there was a faint outline where her hand had rested.

Each evergreen, leaning from the slope at a crazy angle, was more scrawny and lonely than the last. Soon there were only rocks and brush. Then they came to a steep bend called Jacob's Ladder. The wheels seemed to dig deeper into the mountainside. Lynn could not help noticing Vicky: She took a shallow, terrified breath and immediately turned her face from the view.

The return trip was even worse for her. The passengers rode facing bottom, pitched forward. Vicky braced her feet against the floor and clutched the seat, convinced the cogs were going to lose their grip and the train would run away like a roller coaster. But they made it. Somehow.

* * *

43

Lynn woke with a start as someone tugged at her shoulder. It was Nan. They were parked in front of her grandmother's house.

She tried to shake the slumber from her eyes. "What time is it?" When they started for home, it was near dusk.

"Nine-thirty." Nan gestured to Skip and Vicky curled together in the rear. "They're out for the night. Why don't I leave the kittens with you? That is, if you don't mind feeding them before you go to bed."

"Oh sure," Lynn mumbled.

After whispered good-byes and thanks, Lynn tumbled out the door. The headlights, enormous, unblinking eyes, stared at her for a moment. Lynn waved, and the yellow beams bounced over the unpaved track and disappeared.

She yawned several times, trying to defog her head. Grammer's door was pulled to. Lynn ambled into the kitchen, wondering when the kittens had eaten last and how long she could stay awake.

The box was gone. Grammer probably had them in with her. She smiled to herself. What a great day it had been.

Lynn turned off the living room light so she would not awaken Grammer when she opened the door. She waited a few minutes for her eyes to adjust to the dark, then stole into the room.

The bed was as smooth and as empty as it had been when she helped Grammer make it up in the morning. And there was no box.

"Grammer?"

Maybe Grammer was upstairs. Lynn took the steps two at a time. She was not there either.

Now Lynn tore through the farmhouse. Closets, bath-

44

rooms, upstairs and down. The dirt basement. The canning cellar. The pantry. Nowhere. Grammer. Or the kittens. The attic. Nowhere.

She raced outside to the barn. Grammer's ancient gray Dodge still there. No one inside. She slammed the car door. The tack room. Empty cow stalls. Smoke's stall.

Lynn roused the horse and slipped on his bridle. She had no idea where she was going but she had this awful, choking feeling she had better hurry. "Go, Smoke!" she urged.

She searched headlong at first, then more systematically, combing Deerhill Road and each connecting road and path for what must have been hours. Finally, she halted Smoke on one of the bridle paths to the pond. They had traveled it many times already. "Come on, pony boy. You need a drink."

Smoke, hoof deep, lapped at the water. Lynn dismounted to get a closer look at something in the pond.

There was the box — the box Vicky had yielded with such misgiving. She recognized the lettering on the side. The carton bobbed in the water washing the shore line, then sagged drunkenly in the sand. Now it was Lynn who braced herself to prevent the train from hurtling out of control.

7

❦❦❦

Lynn clutched the water-soaked carton. She wanted to go to the Seymours', but how would she explain the missing kittens to Vicky? And what if Nan or Doug were to call her parents?

Soft waves skidded across the pond from the southwest. The box might have drifted from the island. Lynn called out over the water several times. "Hel-lo. Grammer, if you hear me, answer. Hel-lo."

Then she thought she saw something struggle in the black pond. Every nerve was straining to make it out when she remembered the Seymours' canoe. Don't let it be too late, she pleaded silently, as she ran to the guest house.

A metal chain jangled. The blasted thing was locked. Lynn dropped against the steps. The back of her hand throbbed from a scrape on a cinder block. Her chest was bursting, trying to contain the panic that stalked her.

Smoke had followed her to the guest house. He nudged her shoulder. "We have to get help, pony boy," she said, caressing the wide, velvety neck.

The Seymours' cottage was pitch black. Lynn hesitated, then rapped. She waited forever. "Come on, come on," she whispered fiercely. She was pounding now. She was about to try the door handle, when Smoke whinnied softly

46

from his place in the yard. Lynn turned to see what it was.

"Lynn? I thought I heard you calling," said Grammer. "What are you doing here?" Her grandmother appeared beside Smoke like a visitor from the spirit world.

After all she had worried and imagined, Lynn was afraid to speak. "Are you all right?" she managed.

Grammer's voice was thin and fragile. "No, I don't believe I am," and her uncertain body sank.

Lynn rushed to Grammer's side. Light flooded the yard. Soon they were surrounded by the Seymours. Skip and Vicky fetched water and a washcloth, while Doug carefully installed Grammer in a chaise.

"I thought I'd be steadier closer to the ground," said Grammer. She looked around, as if expecting a grin at least, but no one was laughing.

Lynn's grandmother lay back. When she opened her eyes, she tilted her head toward Nan. Nan moved to the foot of the lounge chair to give her an easier view. Grammer moistened her lips. "You know the manner I've kept myself." Nan nodded yes. "If you do understand — please — take me home."

"Of course," Nan replied.

Nan took Lynn aside while Doug was helping Grammer into the car. "My guess is she's okay for now. Try to get her to rest, and — " She took Lynn's hand and started over. "Has she had dizzy spells, maybe blackouts, before? Headaches? Severe headaches, I mean."

"I — " Lynn felt the warm hand holding hers. Nan and Doug were so different from her family, so careful not to blunder into the private places. It hurt to lie to them. "I

47

don't think so." Suddenly Lynn felt her nose sting. She blinked furiously. "Do you think something is wrong?"

Nan searched Lynn's face. "Probably nothing that can't wait until morning. You'll call us if you need anything?"

Lynn blinked some more. "Okay."

The drive home was mercifully short. Grammer and Lynn sat silent. Lynn was petrified that Doug would suggest bringing home the kittens, but not even he made any efforts at conversation. Lynn had smacked Smoke on the rump and hollered, "Home!" Within minutes of their arrival the horse ambled toward Grammer's barn.

"G'night," Doug yawned.

" 'Bye. Thanks," said Lynn, relieved he had not remembered.

Lynn helped her grandmother undress and climb into bed. The wicker chair by the window rustled as she settled on the cushion. Grammer's clothes were completely dry. Lynn couldn't shake the surprise she felt.

After a time, Grammer coughed and sat up. "Child?"

"Yes?" Lynn turned away from the windowsill.

"Do you know where they are?"

"The kittens? Oh, they're in the kitchen." She tried to sound casual.

"Don't protect me, child!" Grammer snapped angrily. "You'll make me think my mind is going. I fear that worse than my body giving up."

"I found the box in the water."

"Oh."

"You don't know?"

"I can't remember. Truly." Grammer fiddled with her blanket. "You and those city people would be home

48

shortly. I figured I'd carry the kittens back. So I followed the beach path. I tired, I reckon. When I was setting at the water's edge, the box alongside me, I knew I was going to have to decide what to do about them — then and there. Just like before."

"Before?"

Her voice dropped almost to nothing. "I may have drowned them."

Maybe Lynn *had* seen something in the water.

"Their kittens look like housecats, if you don't know the difference. We called them bobcats because of the way they run, their behinds rocking up and down. In hard winters, when the wildcats couldn't get rabbits, they followed the deer. They'd eat carrion mostly, but they could jump a live deer, and ride it till it bled to death.

"A few months back I heard them yowling. Mating, most likely. Lordy, they were a peck of trouble. My father and my grandfather used to trap them. No one's seen bobcats in years, but I knew they were back. Can't mistake that sound. Best thing is to drown them." Her voice turned bossy. "No sense in keeping alive what isn't useful. It's the law of the farm."

Nothing she was saying made sense. "Go to sleep, Grammer," Lynn begged, squeezing back tears. "You're tired out of your mind."

Grammer seemed to consider the idea, then rambled on. "There aren't the farms there used to be. But I've as good as gone and done it, haven't I?" Her voice deflated like a punctured bag. "Lordy, I am tired."

Afraid to leave her, Lynn stretched out on the braided rug. Each time she came to, she was aware that her grand-

49

mother slept fitfully as well. After a while, there was not much point in trying to go back to sleep. She sat in the wicker chair, watching daylight fill the window.

Lynn pulled the afghan tighter around her neck. Grammer must have forgotten to take her pills again. Maybe they were not the right pills, not strong enough. A few right pills, please. Teeny white ones, so small no one would notice.

If only that were all it would take.

"Do you want me to call Daddy?" Lynn asked Grammer at breakfast.

"What for? To tell him I'm going dotty?"

She wished Grammer had said yes for once.

Vicky squeezed the sand in between her bare toes. It was cold and slimy. She had not been able to fall back asleep after the commotion with old Mrs. Davis, so at first light she pulled a faded sweatshirt over her nightgown and padded bleary-eyed down to the pond. She still was puzzled by what had happened. Why would Mrs. Davis appear at their house — in the middle of the night? And who knocked at the door? Nan was no help. All she would say was Mrs. Davis was not feeling well and she hoped nothing happened, for Lynn's sake — whatever that meant. Nan was great at cryptic statements.

She just wished the rest of the world would wake up so they could get the kittens.

The damp sand did not make an inviting roost. Vicky was headed for a sun-washed log beside the trees, when a grayish object came to life among the underbrush. Ugh. She had forgotten there were all sorts of miserable creatures on the loose at daybreak.

As she was rolling her log toward the water, something made her look closer. That was no ugly creature. That was a kitten!

Hers!

She found the second kitten not far from the first and stormed to the cottage. All the while she was fixing sweet milk, she ranted and wailed over what that *awful* woman had done, not caring a whit whom she stirred from bed with her anger. It did not help to have Skip return from the beach later with shreds of cardboard and a soggy blue doll blanket, the one they had used to line the box.

Even big-hearted Skip didn't have much to say in her defense.

Nan attempted to make it as easy on Lynn as possible, but the phone call was awkward, nonetheless. When she mentioned that the kittens were safe, she said something like she was sure her grandmother must have been worried.

"Lynn, I think maybe she ought to see a doctor. It may be a very simple thing to treat. Or it could be serious, in which case, she shouldn't wait. I'd be glad to drive her," said Nan.

"No, really. She has pills. She forgot to take them. It only happens when she forgets."

"Are you sure?"

Lynn gritted her teeth. Right now she was not sure of a thing, not of Grammer, of herself, or how she had gotten into this mess. "Yes," she lied. She had never felt so lonely in her whole life.

After the phone call, Lynn changed into her riding boots and went out to the barn. Shivers of excitement riffled Smoke's withers. "Good boy, good boy," she whispered.

The meadow sometimes could be slippery with dew. Lynn reined him in crossing to the abandoned logging trail, and Smoke answered in bright measured steps, as if they moved in an ordered, untroubled world.

The trail looked dry. She guided Smoke onto the khaki soil, then leaned into him. "Now, Smoke! Everything you got."

Her brother and father were driving into Wolfeboro for the Fourth of July parade without Vicky. "Who wants to watch a bunch of rickety volunteer firemen? They can't even keep step," she said. Besides, Vicky was furious — furious with Mrs. Davis and simply broiling at her father, who, without knowing a thing, rose late and declared it was time to stop cooing over the kittens as if they were at death's door. To prove it he placed a shallow bowl of milk, not even sweet milk, in the corner of their new box. And then he had the nerve to give them Mrs. Davis's names.

"Which one's Evinrude?" he said.

Skip pointed to a kitten. "That one. The boy."

Doug turned the kitten over and checked the critical anatomy. "Is this still Evinrude?" Skip nodded.

"No."

"Two to one, Vick." Doug dipped a finger in the milk and tapped the kitten's forehead. "I hereby dub you Evinrude, Knight of the Loyal Order of the Outboard." Skip giggled. "And you — " The second kit was protesting fiercely. "I hereby pronounce you Cleo, First Lady of the Order of Mi-aow." Then the two of them, Doug and

Skip, miaowed and snorted and snickered until it was positively disgusting. Vicky was glad when it was done and they left.

She scratched the side of the box. The kittens oriented to the sound quickly, their eyes bright and penetrating. Cleo pushed up on her front legs. Her rear legs spread like the camel whose behind never wanted to follow its front. Vicky lifted the kitten. After running several steps the legs disbanded again. Vicky stroked the kitten's downy fur. "I bet that crazy old lady killed your mother."

8

❦❦❦

"Looks like you got it fixed," Lynn said, squinting into the sunlight. She had been out for an aimless walk, when she ran into Howie on the beach. "You haven't been around for a while. Was it the carburetor?"

"Yeah," said Howie. "This is the first day I've been on the bike since it went in the mud." Howie revved the engine, then let the sound fade to a low rumble. His face shone with pleasure. "We re-jetted the carb." Lynn looked at him quizzically. "So it'll go faster," he explained, and to demonstrate he revved to a shrill peak.

"Where are your friends?"

"Chris and Joe will be here pretty soon. I got tired of cruising in low so I told them I'd meet them."

With that Howie buzzed the parking lot a couple of times, stopping at the trash container. He fished out several cans and arranged them in a line on the ground. Howie rolled his moped backward a few feet, then, gunning the engine, he charged at the first can. At the last possible moment, he stood and pulled up hard on the handlebars and dropped the front wheel. The can skittered into the weeds.

Howie backed up again and charged the next can. This time the front wheel landed in a direct hit and the can exploded. Quickly he charged the remaining soda cans. Bang! Bang! Each explosion was a cross between a homerun hit and a bloated paper sack popped in the lunchroom. Howie made a victory sweep of the parking lot, leaning deep into the curves, and swung in front of Lynn. "Hey, I owe you a ride."

Howie was considerate: He took the turns slowly and didn't attempt any stunts. "I can't wait till I get mine," Lynn said when she hopped off.

"A ped?" Howie regarded her with a mixture of curiosity and admiration.

"Lots of girls have them."

"Oh sure. Well, when you get it, make it a good one. Used bikes can get pretty beat, and those kind are always letting a guy down. I bought mine from a friend of my brother's." Howie broke off. "Are you going to get one new, or used?" he asked, realizing he may have jumped to conclusions.

"I don't know yet. It depends."

"Yeah, the bucks. I got the money for mine hunting."

"Hunting what?"

He made a ghoulish face. "Escaped convicts, and I col-

54

lect the reward. Dead or alive. Mostly dead — heh heh heh."

"Cut it out." Lynn laughed. "Come on — hunting what?"

Howie leered. "Little animals with fur." He was enjoying Lynn's reaction.

"Oh gross." Lynn turned up her nose, but she could not resist hearing more. "With a gun?"

"Nah. We trap them — and my brother does the rest. He knows a place that buys the skins."

"And you get money for it?"

"What else?"

"How much?"

"Enough to buy my moped."

"I think it's sick," said Lynn.

"What's sick about it?"

"I don't know — killing innocent animals."

"I'm not killing innocent animals," Howie protested.

"Maybe not you — " Oh, what was the use? Suddenly the whole thing had soured. He probably was lying the same way she had — just to grab a little attention. "Hey, I gotta go. My grandmother's all alone. I don't like to leave her."

"Suit yourself." She could tell he was miffed.

Lynn scuffed along the water line, ignoring the Seymours' beach path, and continued to the cove where she was hidden by trees. She sat sloshing the water with her bare feet. She didn't care about Howie. Why had she lied about getting a moped?

A while later, new voices drifted from the beach. Probably Howie's friends Chris and Joe. More soda cans burst. A woman, children yelling, a puppy. If only she had the

55

guts to walk back to the Seymours' beach path, the guts to
be honest. But she couldn't even do that with Howie.

Some Davis.

Lynn opened the door to the front porch. She looked
out the screen. Seeing them gave her a start. It had been
days. "Hi," she said weakly.

"We're going blackberry picking. Want to join us?"
said Nan.

Every time Lynn had fantasied getting back together
with them, the meeting was awkward and difficult. This
seemed almost too easy. But here they were. She was
elated. "Let me tell my grandmother."

"She's invited, too," said Nan. When Grammer agreed
to come along, Lynn was surprised, but pleased. It was
right somehow that she should be included in a reunion
with the Seymours.

The blackberry patch was such a popular spot a small
circle had been trampled through the dense growth, and
the easiest fruit to reach was picked already, although a
few glossy berries were left to tempt them.

Vicky dived into the brambles after them, but the
prickers stung, and disturbing the shrubs aroused the
mosquitoes. "No fair. Why do they only come to me?"
Vicky waved and slapped her arms to scare them away, but
there was no relief.

"I can't stand this. Here." She handed her bucket to
Lynn and in a frenzy fled the thicket to roll in the grass
nearby.

When Nan and Lynn and Skip stopped, they had barely
enough berries for tomorrow's breakfast. "I recall bushes
farther on," said Grammer, directing them down the

slope. "It used to be some of the best berry-picking around. Can't see it from the road, so you had to know it's there."

"Great!" Skip whooped.

"Vick, you're bitten up enough already. You stay here."

They hiked off and Grammer remained behind with Vicky. The polite thing to do would be to talk. Vicky cleared her throat a couple of times, warming up, as it were, but Mrs. Davis seemed intent on keeping silent. She sunned her face and once or twice bent to pluck a stalk of grass and examine it. What she saw that interested her so much Vicky had no idea.

After the disaster with the kittens, Nan and Vicky had talked a lot, with Vicky's rage petering out in words, though she hid a small reserve — in case the need arose. Rationally, she had to agree with her mother: Yes, leaving the kittens probably was an accident; yes, the mother cat probably had been hit on the highway, but, looking at Mrs. Davis's uneven and complicated face, she could not be satisfied this was the whole story.

"Haven't you ever seen one before?" Mrs. Davis asked.

"Huh?" Vicky scratched at her legs.

"A decrepit person. The way you were staring, I thought maybe I was your first."

Vicky blushed. "Oh, sorry. No. I mean yes, I have seen one. My great-aunt Rae. She had a stroke and she has to use a cane. But she would never say she was decrepit."

"No? Why not?"

"Because she doesn't think she is."

"But you think she is."

"No, she's old, but not decrepit."

57

Mrs. Davis lifted an eyebrow. "I see. So decrepit is something besides counting years. How do you suppose your aunt has escaped becoming decrepit?"

"Maybe because she can still do the things she likes to do. She lives near Washington, and she's always writing letters to Congress and going to visit their offices and everything. She says she's waiting to vote for the first woman President. I told her I'd try for it. In school I'm going to run for Student Council. I already have somebody lined up to nominate me."

"Then you'll have to work on developing a firm hand-shake. People like a strong, neighborly hand — gives them confidence. Let me feel yours." Vicky put out a hand and shook the way she imagined it ought to be done; she wasn't accustomed to shaking hands, except occasionally when her father brought home visiting lecturers or gradu-ate students. "Well," Lynn's grandmother said, "I'd vote for someone with a hand like yours."

Vicky released Mrs. Davis's papery hand, aware of what the old woman's grip had spoken of her.

Then they chatted. Even their disagreements were friendly. Vicky said her first project as a student govern-ment representative was going to be to introduce an equal rights amendment. Her aunt Rae had been a friend of Alice Paul's, the original organizer for the ERA. Mrs. Davis harumphed. "That's where we part company," she said. "I don't ask for special favors."

"But that's not a favor," Vicky argued. "We're enti-tled."

Their wait had passed quickly. The others arrived and displayed a full bucket of berries — "black caps" Mrs. Davis called them — and they returned home. Lynn's grandmother begged off on the pie-baking. Before she closed the car door, she gave Vicky a special nod in the back seat. Vicky watched the thick-heeled shoes, the cottony stockings, the print dress; they were sturdy, practical. Vicky recalled the feel of her hand. It was hard to believe someone with a hold like that could do something as — well, decrepit — as misplacing two kittens in a large box.

Vicky twisted the bottom of her T-shirt over the hot red welts circling her waist. "Lookit. Even on my stomach."

"Think about something else," her mother ordered, as she applied a baking-soda-and-water paste to the mosquito bites. "What did you and Mrs. Davis talk about today?"

"Aunt Rae, mostly."

"They should have a lot in common — both very independent women."

"But I don't know if they'd like each other. They'd argue a lot, that's for sure."

Nan was amused at the thought. "Still angry with Mrs. Davis?"

"Not really." Even Vicky's reserve anger was about gone. "Mom? Do you know Lynn's mother?"

"Not well," said Nan. "I never wanted to know her better, to be honest. She never seemed quite real to me. Every hair in place — that sort of thing." Nan held Vicky's arm. "Don't itch."

"The next time I go berry-picking it's going to be at the fruit stand."

Nan knelt on the floor and dabbed Vicky's leg. Vicky started to laugh. "I know this tickles, Victoria, but you simply have got to hold still."

"No, it's Cleo." Vicky pointed. In the corner beneath

the sink Cleo was curled in the pie pan they used to catch drips. Cleo opened one eye a slit, made a few unambitious stabs at licking a paw, and promptly returned to sleep. "Cleopatra pie," Vicky giggled.

Just then Lynn barged into the kitchen. "I brought Smoke down. Let's give it another try," she called to Vicky.

"Do I have to?" It was a half-hearted protest.

"You sound like Skip. Go play equestrian," Nan said, giving one of Vicky's mosquito bites a last swipe. She winked to Lynn. "I think it's good for Vick to face something she doesn't do well. Maybe she'll be more sympathetic to her brother."

"Skip doesn't do well because he doesn't try. Come on, Lynn." Vicky marched out the door, wearing a grimly superior look.

Nan chuckled. "The pie will be ready in about an hour."

After Vicky's boastful exit it was embarrassing to be led around and around in the front yard in full view of her mother, but Lynn was insistent that posture was all important. Lynn tugged at her knees and elbows.

"Don't. That makes it worse."

"You're tight. You have to relax. Here and here."

"How can I, when I'm scared to death I'll fall?" said Vicky.

"It's not that high."

"Wanna bet? What I need is a horse with very short legs and a seatbelt."

"And an insurance policy," Lynn retorted good-naturedly. "I don't get it," she said, walking alongside.

"How can somebody who wants to be president of student gov' be afraid of horses? You have to make speeches, run meetings. For me, that would be scary."

"Telling people what you think is easy. You just say it."

"I don't know. For some people, I guess." Lynn forced herself to concentrate on Vicky's riding. "You're hunching over again. Roll with the movement. Don't fight it." Vicky was trying, but her fear drew in her head and shoulders as though they were on a purse string. Lynn imagined it was the way she must look when she lied to her mother.

"Hey, I'm sorry," said Lynn, "about what happened to the kittens. My grandmother didn't really — "

Vicky interrupted. "It's not your fault. Anyway, I think your grandmother and I are friends now."

"You talked about it?"

"No, not exactly. We talked about other stuff. But we shook hands."

"Aay, neat," said Lynn. "I knew you'd hit it off if you had the chance."

They did one more turn around the circle. "Why do you always say 'I don't know' and 'I'm sorry'?" Vicky asked. "You do it all the time, like apologizing for your grandmother."

Lynn blurted out laughing, "I don't know."

"My Aunt Rae says it's a bad habit. It's excusing yourself before you make a mistake, and she says people should have the guts to commit themselves to an opinion and fall flat on their faces once in a while," Vicky recited, a little too smug.

Why bother having opinions, thought Lynn, when nobody except your grandmother cares about them? She stifled the urge to preface her answer with another "I don't know." "She has a point," said Lynn. That was hardly an opinion, but it was not an apology.

Nan stepped out the kitchen door. "Blackberry pie! Homemade!" she sang. Skip came dashing from the beach path and Lynn ran to the house behind him.

"Hey, get me down from here!" Vicky yelled.

Lynn stood in the doorway. She cupped her hands over her mouth. "And I'm not sorry."

Vicky laughed. "Hold the door open. I'm going to ride him in."

9

❧❧❧

The badminton birdie hung for a moment in midair, then dropped beyond Lynn's racket. From out of nowhere Rudy dashed after it, touching nose first to the white feathers. He bounced sideways as if they were live.

Lynn put down her racket to watch. Rudy and Cleo were big enough now to be fun, more than she'd guessed they could be. They scampered after anything: insects, stray pieces of paper, even a toe jiggling in a sandal. One cat would dart at the other, rear and paw like a toy horse, then scoot away, and when the second cat caught him, they clambered and rolled until it was impossible to distinguish heads from tails.

Vicky stomped to where Rudy was playing and scooped him into her arms. "Skip! He's out again."

"I think maybe I did it when I went in to get a new birdie," said Lynn.

"Aww, what difference does it make?" said Skip.

"Plenty. They could get slammed in a door or stepped on — or run over."

"The mail truck's the only thing that goes by here."

"That's not true. There are cars on the road to the beach. And what about the highway?"

"They don't go that far. They're too little."

"They will some day," Vicky threatened.

"You're as bad as Harp the Carp," muttered Skip. "You never want anybody to have fun."

Skip's remark jolted Vicky. "They practically died," she defended herself. She looked to Lynn for support, but Lynn sided with Skip.

Rudy meanwhile was wriggling from Vicky's hold. She let go grudgingly.

He crouched in the daylilies and immediately was absorbed in Smoke's tail. Each time the tail switched, so did Rudy's little head. Back and forth. Rudy was snaking along the porch. Back and forth. Beside a rock. Back and forth.

Back and forth.

And — leap! Rudy flew at the tail.

Smoke threw his rear legs, his hooves barely missing the cat. The pair split in opposite directions: Smoke toward the pond, Rudy to the crawlspace under the porch.

Vicky laughed heartily, then sighed. "All right, you win. But I am not Harp the Carp."

It was getting on toward five o'clock, time to be heading

home. Lynn decided to detour to Grammer's by way of the cove. Usually in the late afternoon the sluggish marsh area came alive with a flurry of activity. Birds swooped on smaller prey, or they quarreled over half-eaten sandwiches. Nearby, the rabbits hopped from weed to weed, delicately chewing the heads and leaving the stems standing like thin soldiers. Today Lynn sensed an uneasy quiet. The animals must have been frightened away.

Then rounding the bend, she saw why. There were Howie and his two friends. Nothing obvious was wrong, but their being in that particular place — and the way they jumped on their bikes when they saw her — made Lynn wonder. Howie, eyes dodging as they passed, barely said hello.

Over dinner Lynn asked Grammer if she knew anything about Howie and his pals.

"I wouldn't be surprised if they're the same fellows I ran off one day last winter. One of them's got dark hair, hangs in his eyes? And a blond chunky thing with a big space between his two front teeth. Can't remember what the third one looked like. That sound like the ones you know?"

Lynn shook her head yes. "The dark one is Howie."

"He was the talker. Ay-uh. Had quite the run-in with them."

"About what?" Lynn stopped buttering her steamy biscuit.

"I caught them prowling behind the barn. You get hunters on occasion, they can't read NO TRESPASSING signs. I toted my rifle in case anyone thought I didn't mean business. Felt downright foolish, when I found it was kids." Grammer chuckled. "Scared the ever-living lights out of them, I'll tell you."

"What did they want?"

"Darned if I know. I saw them from the house again a couple of weeks later, but I was feeling so poorly by then I had to call Hazel Reidy's son Robert to chase them off. I swear they got into the barn. It didn't appear they bothered anything. Just boyish mischief," said Grammer.

After dinner they sat on the front porch. This was the hour Lynn enjoyed best, listening to the approaching night sounds, watching night steal the last of the day's shimmering gold and blood-orange afterlight and turn it to shadow.

Their after-supper ritual was broken by the telephone. Lynn knew who it was before she picked up the receiver. "Hello?"

"We miss you, darling."

"Hi, Mom. Everything's fine."

"Good," she said, her voice bright and enthusiastic. "What have you been doing with yourself?"

So that's why she called. Lynn thought her mother had sounded upset when she heard how much time she was spending with Vicky and Skip. "I met some boys." It wasn't a total lie. There was Howie.

"How nice. Your age?"

There it was. "Yeah, I think so. I met them on the beach."

"Wonderful, dear. Where are they from?"

Lynn thought fast. "Boston."

"Now you can have some real fun. Is your grandmother eating?"

65

"Sure."

"Older people often lose interest in food and forget to prepare meals. I don't want you living on snacks. It's bad for your complexion." Lynn tuned out while her mother droned. Finally she could hang up.

"What's old nose-box want?" Grammer called from the porch.

Lynn smiled. There were times when Grammer knew exactly the right thing to say. She banged the screen door. "The usual. This time it was balanced meals."

"Ha," Grammer snorted.

"Makes me want to eat a whole box of Marshmallow Jingles."

"We got any left?" Grammer asked slyly.

"Oh, you don't know a Marshmallow Jingle from a Devil Donut."

Grammer frowned. "You didn't tell her, did you?"

"About what?"

"Oh — my foolishness, at the pond — all that business," she answered a little too lightly.

"No."

"Good." She repeated it. "Good."

The truth was Lynn had forgotten. Well, not forgotten, but she had pretty much stopped worrying. The first few days she half expected Grammer to collapse any moment. But when nothing happened, she was more and more convinced Grammer had not taken her pills.

The two of them worked in Grammer's garden and drove her shiny 1962 Dodge to Old Home Day fairs and flea markets, the normal routine. Lynn just kept a sharper eye on the medicine. She persuaded Grammer to store her bottle on the breakfast table, where she would remember to take it — and where Lynn could easily count tablets without Grammer's knowing.

When Lynn looked up, Grammer had slipped inside. She spent a few minutes watching an unruly wind play on the weathervane, then followed her grandmother in.

"Storm tonight." Grammer shivered, closing the book in her lap.

"What's that?" said Lynn.

"My picture album. The book's half empty and I've got a mess of pictures sitting in cooky tins. Time I put them in order."

The album was oversized with raised bumps on the black cover. Her grandmother flipped the sheets. Crisp white corners tacked the photographs in place. Grammer adjusted her reading glasses and tilted her head as if to read through her nose, then pointed to a slight man with round spectacles. He wore suspenders and carried a hat. "Here's your Grandfather Davis, shortly after we were married." He had died after a fall from a hay wagon; that was about as much as Lynn knew.

"He looks old," said Lynn, trying to find a resemblance to her father.

"A man waited till he could afford a wife then. Had ourselves a fancy Florida honeymoon. Two days each way on the train. Your grandfather was a real train man."

Grammer smiled at something remembered. "My, but the fish dressed fine — all colors — not like the homely things we have here. They had alligators, too, One chased lickety-split out of the water after your grandfather." She laughed. "Almost had a taste of Yankee pride."

Grammer moistened a finger and leafed through the pages. "Here he is again." The woman on his arm wore an eyelet dress gathered softly with a ribbon and a spray of flowers caught in her hair.

Lynn glanced quickly between the picture and her grandmother. "Is that you?"

"Wouldn't know it, would you," Grammer said proudly.

"You were pretty."

"We'd won the state square dance competitions. That's how we met, challenge dancing. We swapped partners and didn't quit dancing until he was taken from me." She gave Lynn a friendly jab. "How about you? Someone you're mushy over, back home?"

How could she explain people didn't get "mushy" anymore? "There's one guy I talk to a lot. Homework mostly. We're just friends."

Grammer examined Lynn closely. "Sounds boring, if you ask me." She peered through her nose again, pointing to a picture of two starched and dour women. "Those are the Davis sisters. Pew-hugging crows, the both of them. Never lifted a finger except to nag and crochet."

A picture on the opposite page caught Lynn's attention. Her grandmother and grandfather were sitting in wooden lawn chairs. The Davis sisters stood in the shade of the porch behind them, and in the foreground a baby in a sailor suit crawled between two large cats. They could have been small tigers.

Lynn was about to take a closer look at the baby — he would have been her father — when Grammer brusquely turned the page. "Well. You've seen it all. I'll have to get busy, paste in the others." Her hands curled together over the book.

It could have been her mother switching off the TV in

the middle of a good program. Maybe that was why Lynn said what she did. "My best friend's grandfather died, and her grandmother got married again." Lynn knew how preposterous the suggestion was.

"When I pass to my reward, I'll go as a Davis, none other. I look forward to joining up with Gerald, I do, but maybe the good Lord saw fit to shelter his sisters in another place," she cackled softly.

Suddenly Grammer hiked up the hem of her dress. "Look at these — " she said, as she flexed her bare ankles. "They don't look seventy-nine."

Lynn stared, embarrassed at first. She was right. They were firm, shapely legs.

"But my face sags and I'm speckled as a brown hen." She tapped the age spots on her hands and her face. "Child, you don't know how mixed up it is — parts of yourself old, and parts not. It isn't a hundred percent one or the other, at least not yet. A man dies. You go on working and doing whatever else you have to do, until one day you wake up in a seventy-nine-year-old body, and you realize your mind is twenty years behind.

"I wonder if Mr. Davis will recognize me on the other side. When you die, do you sort of freeze up where you are, or does a body continue getting older? What if he's froze in one place and I'm in another?"

"I don't know," Lynn said with a shrug. Debbie's grandmother didn't talk like this. She got married was what she wanted to say. Grammer forgot her pills again. Lynn was sure of it.

"Look at this," Skip hollered to Vicky. He carried Rudy to the screened porch and yanked a clump of fur.

Vicky was still smarting from his comparing her to Mrs. Harper. "Don't! You'll hurt him, you dope. What did you do that for?" She reached to take Rudy from Skip.

"No, look. It's coming out in bunches. And feel. Underneath." He pressed Vicky's hand into Rudy's coat. "The new fur's real stiff."

"So?"

"Don't you think it's weird?"

"Why should I?"

"It's not like a regular cat. Regular cats don't lose their baby fur like that. And regular fur isn't so hard."

Rudy squeezed and stretched his claws, rumbling contentedly in Vicky's lap. "Their paws are big, too. And their tails aren't growing. See how short it is?" said Skip, lifting Rudy's rump.

Rudy's tail did not look short to her. "You're making it up. You don't know anything about cats."

"I do so. Jimmy Porter has two of them."

"One died."

"He had two."

"That doesn't make you an expert."

"Vicky! Skip! Help!" Nan called from the living room. It sounded like trouble. Vicky put Rudy aside, while Skip led the way.

Books lay scattered across the floor. Their mother was spread-eagled against the bookcase. Nan twisted to speak over her shoulder. "I kept hearing this plop! plop! It's Cleo. Heaven only knows how she got up there." She was laughing so hard the tears were flowing.

"Where?" said Skip, looking at the half-empty shelf, then at the floor.

"In back of the books."

Two yellow orbs peeped out of the darkness above Nan's head and quickly retreated. Several books inched forward on the shelf. One or two were threatening to topple until Nan managed to nudge them into place. The eyes flashed again.

"She's discovered a dark, cozy spot, but every time she turns to settle down, she knocks off more books."

"Maybe she thinks she's building a nest," offered Skip.

"See if you can get her," Nan giggled, "before she drops any more of her nest on my head."

Skip climbed the back of the overstuffed chair beside the bookcase. "She must have jumped from here," said Skip.

"Uh-oh," said Vicky. "She didn't fly, that's for sure." Vicky gestured behind the chair.

Nan dropped her arms to look. One panel of the lace curtains was snagged and misshapen, as if a clumsy weight had clung to it. Nan had been so pleased the day she found them at a flea market.

"Ow!" Skip yelled. "Bad cat!" Cleo fled from the room. "She bit me," said Skip, as much stunned as angry. "Hard."

Late that evening Lynn bent over the kitchen table, counting.

"Seems to me, your mother isn't the only nose-box," said a voice in the semidarkness behind her.

10

❧❧❧

The sun was just beginning to penetrate the cool morning air. Except for the cats, Vicky and Skip had the beach to themselves. Vicky tipped a brown leaf with her toe and thought about wading out to Skull, a massive stone rising from the pond like the petrified head of a woolly mammoth, maybe half a short city block from shore. It made an ideal spot for daydreaming.

She was ready to toss her terry robe on the sand when Rudy approached the water. Without any hesitation, he simply stepped in and lapped. Soon Cleo waded in for a drink, too.

"Skip, do you see?" Vicky whispered.

Skip let out a whistle. "Cats hate water. Don't they?" he added.

She didn't know why, but she was excited. They were *in* the water, lapping, no hurry, until they had had enough. And they didn't seem to mind!

Finished, Rudy stepped gingerly out of the pond, shaking each paw. Droplets glistened like sequins on his amber-and-gray fur. Both animals settled under the bushes at the edge of the beach and licked and licked, between their toes, the pads of their feet, their ears, their faces, their tan underbellies. Without their baby fuzziness they were so much longer and sleeker.

"This can't be the first time they've been down here for

water," said Vicky. "They knew exactly what they were doing. Probably they got desperate. Somebody's always forgetting to fill their water bowl."

"It's your job, too."

Vicky ignored the protest. "I wonder how far in they'll go."

"Whaddya mean? Like swimming? Cats can't swim."

"Yes, they can. I read it somewhere. They don't like to, but they can. I want to take them out in the canoe and let them swim back."

"They'll drown!"

"Cats can swim," she answered firmly. "We'll take them out a little way. As far as Skull."

"I think it's mean."

"They went in by themselves, didn't they? You saw them."

"I guess so," Skip admitted.

"I know. You take them out. I'll call from here. If they have any trouble swimming, you can pull them in."

"You do it. I'm not helping."

"You'll be right there."

"It's mean," grumbled Skip, but he obediently lifted Cleo and Rudy into the canoe and pushed it ahead of him to the rock.

Vicky stood on shore, making smooching noises and calling, "Here kitty, here kitty." On the rock the cats paced. A couple of times Rudy edged toward the water, but each time he rotated in a tight circle and returned to the top.

"What did I tell you? I'm bringing them in," yelled Skip.

"No, wait. I'll get the ball." The ball was a fluorescent orange sponge, part of a kiddie tennis set, that Cleo had

73

dragged from under the screened porch. It had become a favorite beach toy. One of them would toss the ball low to the ground, while the cats, their eyes darting, waited for the right moment to pounce and shake it.

The toy sailed through the air to Skip. "Throw it. C'mon, throw it."

Skip shook his head no.

"You just don't want to prove I'm right."

"Oh, all right." Skip threw carelessly. As soon as the cats noticed the ball, they perked up. Vicky returned it. Back and forth it flew, the cats following each pass with keen interest.

Skip stretched for a high throw. He missed and fell backward with a noisy splash.

A second, quieter splash followed. Vicky could hardly believe her eyes. Rudy went into the water! He was paddling toward the ball.

"Let him get it! Let him get it!" Vicky screamed. She leaped and clapped and screamed some more. She could not help herself. Nothing as exciting as this had happened — ever.

Rudy gripped the ball between his teeth and headed for land, his ears folded back, head bobbing above the surface. In a short while he dropped the soggy mass in front of Vicky and slapped it between his paws, splattering water everywhere.

"He wants to play! Oh, look!" Vicky hollered. Cleo was easing herself into the water, too. She swam in sturdy, efficient strokes. "I knew it! I knew they could do it! We've got the smartest cats anywhere!"

* * *

74

Skip came running out of the water and flopped beside Lynn in the sand. "You didn't believe it until you saw it, huh. Bet no one else has cats that swim. I think we should work up an act or something. Get on TV. Man, we could be stars!" Skip scooped a handful of damp sand and tossed it. "Come on. You can try it, too."

Lynn played a half-hearted game of Cat Catch, then made some excuse to go back to her blanket. Nothing seemed to unglue her mind from her grandmother.

Ever since Grammer caught her counting pills she had acted like a stranger. The silences didn't bother Lynn. She was used to those. It was what Grammer said that was different: "Nice day." Or, "Pass the oleo," as if she were sitting on the next stool at a coffee counter in Anonymous, U.S.A. When it happened, Lynn had tried to pretend it was a mindless game, she didn't realize — but her grandmother cut her short. "Somebody getting nose-boxed ought to know not to pass it on."

A few days of this and Lynn couldn't stand it any longer. Maybe she should offer to go home.

Lynn heard loud voices coming from the rock: Vicky and Skip. She almost welcomed another one of their battles as a reason to stop thinking about Grammer.

Winding up first like a propeller, Skip was pretending to throw the ball toward the island, but hid it behind his back instead. "Go get it," he urged Cleo. Cleo's ears flicked between Skip and the island, questioning.

"No fair. You gotta give her the ball," Vicky demanded.

"I just wanted to see what she'd do," he said. Skip pretended to throw again and jumped into the water, chasing the imaginary object. Cleo dropped in behind and paddled past, straight for the island.

Skip stopped swimming. No one said anything. They watched Cleo, expecting her to turn back at any moment, but in a short time her head was barely visible above the water. Lynn was starting to feel uncomfortable.

Suddenly Vicky burst. "Skip Seymour, you get that cat!"

Skip did not argue. He struck out for the island, and Cleo.

Immediately, Lynn launched the canoe. Vicky boarded at the rock and together they guided their craft in the direction they last spotted the cat. They made a good team. The canoe sped.

"There she is!" Vicky's paddle dipped faster.

They overtook Cleo swimming in circles about midway between the island and Skull. Vicky dragged the drenched cat into the boat and hugged her. Then they picked up Skip, who made a shame-faced apology to Cleo. Cleo planted her feet on the bottom of the boat and shook, then preened. It was nothing, she seemed to say.

Sitting erect in the middle of the canoe with the late afternoon sun radiating off her as they glided across the water, there was an otherworldly shimmer about Cleo. On land, majestic pines tipped their crowns to the stately passenger. Whispering oars dipped in awe, while the darning needles buzzed and swooped like courtiers.

The sound of the boat scraping bottom broke the spell.

"I'll get out," volunteered Skip. He splashed over the side and led with the tow rope. Soon the boat thumped again and Lynn and Vicky had to jump out, when Cleo started pacing. Periodically she stopped to stare at the shore, her ears twitching.

"Cleo wants out," said Lynn.

A blue car with enormous tail fins was parked on the service road to the pond. A man and a woman sat sunning themselves nearby. Howie and his friends were there and a family with small children. Nothing unusual, yet Cleo kept pacing.

As soon as they drew ashore, she bounded from the canoe and, dropping her body close to the sand, hurtled up the slope into the underbrush. A short time later a dog yipped, followed by a high-pitched cat's shriek.

"Rudy!"

Lynn, Vicky, and Skip ran up the path.

Lynn stopped. "There they are." She pointed beyond a small clearing. Rudy was crouched on a limb. Cleo was backed against the base of the tree, her paw poised to slash at the dog dancing and barking around the tree trunk.

"He's only a puppy," said Skip. "He wants to play." The dog was a short-haired mongrel with wagging brown ears and a frisky tail. He rushed forward, then retreated, daring Cleo to follow. Her paw stabbed the air.

"Cleo sure doesn't. We better get that dog away from her." Lynn charged, shouting at the dog. "Go home!" The animal turned tail and trotted through the brush.

Skip tried to force Rudy from his perch. He called to him and hit at the tree branch with a fallen limb, but Rudy blinked and refused to budge.

"Do you suppose Cleo knew Rudy was in trouble?" Vicky asked Lynn.

"I don't know. I didn't think cats did that — fight for

each other. A mother cat for her babies, maybe." Lynn shook her head. "I don't know." She picked up Cleo, who was still skittish. "You're one tough cat, Cleopatra. What're you gonna be when you're all grown up?"

"Hey, what's going on?" a cheery voice boomed. "Don't I get a welcome?"

"Daddy!" Skip flew at his father and wrapped him in an extra-tight bear hug. "Are you here for good?"

"Till school starts again. Summer session is over." Doug broke into a singsong, "No more lessons, no more books, no more teacher's dirty looks."

"Daddy, you're the teacher."

"Whoops."

Grammer was staring absent-mindedly out the kitchen window when Lynn returned from the Seymours'. From the darkened hallway she watched Grammer stir herself and hastily water plants hanging in the window.

Lynn opened the refrigerator and poured a glass of milk. She pulled up a chair at the table. "We have to talk," she said, bolder than she felt. She waited for Grammer to turn around, to say something, but she stood silent at the sink. "I think I'd — I'm going home."

The old woman's hand shook so hard water slopped over the top of the pitcher onto the counter. "What for?"

"You know."

Grammer buttoned and unbuttoned the neck of her dress. "The gate's never been locked."

Lynn pushed away from the table. She had been counting on Grammer's telling her not to go. "I'll call Mom and Dad tomorrow. I don't feel like it tonight."

"Take your time."

Was that it? Grammer telling her not to? "It'll be —
uh — weird, you know? Going home in the middle of the
summer," she said, giving her grandmother another
chance.

Grammer pinched a few dead leaves from her Swedish
ivy. Lynn vanished up the hallway.

11

❧❧❧

Vicky and Skip looked up from a lazy game of cards. Lynn
was sitting beside Skip, coaching him.

"Those cats are driving me mad," said Nan, as she
limped to the nearest lawn chair. "They eat our dinner.
They tear the house apart. Meanwhile, I can't work. And
this is the last straw." She pressed a big lump on her shin
that was rapidly turning blue.

"Yesterday Cleo climbs the curtains again and when I
try to get her down, what does she do? She rips off the entire rod! My desk is their playground. Pencils, erasers,
paper clips — on the floor. Rubber bands they chew. I finally get Rudy to leave me alone, and I find cat tracks all
over my clean copy. I was going to send it out today to my
committee."

Uh-oh, thought Vicky, this is bad.

"Charles Seymour, don't you dare laugh. This is not
one bit funny."

"But how did you get the egg?" said Lynn.

Nan's face reddened. "Oh . . . I saw the mess . . . I was yelling. Rudy started running. I got so mad I chased him. I thought I had him cornered there in the walkway to the garage. But he never stopped spinning his wheels. He ran full tilt right at me. Crashed into my leg. Here."

Vicky tried not to laugh, but when Nan guffawed, there was no holding back.

"He's got a tough head." Nan laughed with her. "I found him out by the garden. He's okay. Kids, you've got to help me. I can't study with cats knocking down books and curtains and spending half my life searching for a pen. You've been great this summer. But the cats have got to go."

"Go?"

"Well . . . out. I want the house off-limits to the cats."

"All the time?"

"All the time."

"What if it rains?" said Skip.

"What about the dog?" said Vicky. The brown-and-white mongrel that treed Rudy had come nosing around the Seymours' several times.

"The cats will be safe enough, Vick. They can live in the guest house. From now on you feed them there. And we'll have to keep the doors closed so they don't come in the house."

"The doors to the porch?"

"Yeah, Mom, you gotta let them on the porch."

"Okay," Nan relented, "but only on the porch." She shook her head at Lynn. "What are we going to do when we can't ship them off to the guest house?" — meaning the end of summer and going home to New York. Vicky winced.

Vicky was mulling it over when she and Lynn took Cleo for a ride in the boat.

"The people with the funny car are back," said Lynn. "I wonder how old it is. Sure is ugly."

The two girls backpaddled, slowing the canoe to steal a good look at them. He was growing a beard, which didn't look so scraggly at this distance. She was sort of mousy and always wore the wrong sort of tops for her jeans shorts, blouses with palm trees or parrots, instead of T-shirts. Vicky and Lynn had spied them on the beach one day eating cold soup out of cans and they had been the brunt of a lot of jokes ever since.

"Look who's tied behind the car," said Lynn. It was the brown-and-white dog. He strained at his leash and barked.

"We should have known he was theirs." Vicky reached to scratch Cleo's ears, but Cleo turned her head away. She was more interested in the barking dog. "It's okay, Cleo," Vicky murmured. "We won't let him hurt you."

They paddled away from shore and minutes later they were stepping from rock to rock in the water, pulling the boat behind them onto a bare stretch of the island. Cleo trotted through the slender trees after them to a sunning place on the far side. The cat promptly curled into a ball in a niche between two big rocks and dozed off.

Lynn yawned and rolled over on her stomach. "Cleo's got the right idea. Siesta time." Vicky knew Lynn was only pretending to nap. She seemed down lately. Nan noticed it, too.

Vicky leaned back and watched Cleo. Cleo's tongue was working in her sleep and her ribs swelled irregularly. The dream subsided after a bit and she was still. Nan was right: The cats would be okay in the guest house. But Vicky had this ominous feeling. Not the worry she felt when they were weak and unable to feed themselves. This was different.

Every day Rudy and Cleo looked and behaved more like full-grown cats, sleeping through the heat of the day, then prowling as dark drew close. They had become constant playmates — on the beach, in the canoe.

Yet the more time Vicky spent with them, the more there was something unfamiliar about the cats. Especially Cleo. Doug kidded about how ugly they were. Vicky knew the cats were not ugly, but she understood what he meant. There was an ugly, disquieting side to them.

Like the incidents with the meat. A few days back she and her mother had brought home chuck steaks to barbecue. They were unpacking the steaks, when Cleo jumped onto the counter. Vicky tried to push her away, but she clung stubbornly and in the struggle the meat fell.

Cleo mewed a strange, injured cry and dropped to the floor. Red stains were oozing from the plastic wrap. Both cats nuzzled at it and began to chew their way to the source. Vicky stared.

"Victoria!" Nan grabbed the package. "Put them outside," she ordered, then eyed Vicky suspiciously. "I almost think you wanted them to get it."

That evening her father had started the charcoal in their hibachi. One handle had burned off summers ago, so Doug used two long forks to lower and raise the grate. "White-hot," he said, pleased. Just as he was moving the grid closer to the coals, Cleo bounced up and snagged a raw steak.

Doug laughed. "You old rascal," and he reached for the meat on the ground.

Cleo growled, long and mean, her teeth bared. This was not a game. Surprised, Doug backed off, then reached again. Cleo's claws snapped like a whip, barely missing his cheek.

"Doug, let her have it!" Nan screeched. "Let her have it," she insisted.

Rudy appeared on the run. It was as if the piece of meat were a live animal. The cats snarled and they warbled, they shook, they mouthed it, and they tore at it. These were all things Vicky had seen before, but they no longer seemed playful.

"I think from now on we'd better keep our distance at feeding time," said Nan. "They're too protective of their food."

"If they're so fierce, how come they're sharing?" Vicky asked. Rudy and Cleo really appeared to be taking turns killing the meat. They had growled at the people, not at each other.

"Good question," said Doug, genuinely puzzled.

Then yesterday. Yesterday she and Skip had gone fishing. They stole worms out of Nan's garden, instead of planning ahead and catching nightcrawlers, as they had been told. Maybe it was the wrong time of day, or maybe it was the stolen worms, but the fish were not biting. All they brought up was one dull-colored fish too small to keep and a couple of catfish. The baby fish was easy to release, but Vicky was wary of being stung by the wriggling catfish barbels. Instead of unhooking the fish, she held it behind the head and yanked hard on the line.

Skip paled at the bloody sight. "I'm going to be sick."

"No, you're not," Vicky snapped, trying to hide her own disgust. "You're going to paddle."

"We should have waited for Dad. He knows how to take the fish off without hurting them."

"Paddle!"

The second catfish flopped miserably on Skip's hook. Vicky stopped. "For crying out loud." She pulled off her sneaker and smacked the fish over the head. It jumped feebly a few times, then no more.

"I'm not eating those things. Do we have to clean them if we give them to the cats?" Skip whimpered.

"No."

"Phew."

"But you gotta get the hook out, chicken," said Vicky, having the last word.

After they reached shore, Skip shouldered the pole, his catfish swinging on the end, and tramped up the hill. Vicky finished locking the boat and followed.

He was in the yard calling for the cats. "Here, kitty. Here, kitty, kitty, kitty."

"Skip, look out!" But Vicky cried too late. Skip had not seen Rudy in the lawn chair behind him. When the fish swept past, Rudy extended a claw, raking Skip's arm. Skip howled with surprise.

Blood poured in four irregular streaks down to his wrist. Vicky rushed to quiet him. "Don't bother Mom. Okay?" She patted Skip's wound with a clean tissue she dug out of her pants pocket.

"Why?" said Skip.

"She might not like it, that's all."

"She didn't do anything when Jimmy Porter's cat scratched me. She just said to wash it." Skip thought a minute. "Will you wash it if I don't tell?"

Playing nurse for Skip was a small price to pay for his

silence. Nan was already upset with the cats after the chuck steaks. "Sometimes you're not so dumb, little brother. Yeah, I'll wash it."

Then Rudy had to blow it today by going for a stroll on Nan's thesis. Vicky dropped a hand over the rock to the crevice where Cleo snoozed. The cat purred, lightly bumping her nose against Vicky's outstretched fingers.

"Hey, Vick?" Lynn was talking to her.

"What?"

Lynn's eyes were closed still. "When you get up there to make your speeches, how does it feel? Do you get nervous?"

"Sure. I haven't given too many speeches so far, but I did some for our debate team and one when I had to present the flowers from the school to Mrs. Wendell. She was retiring. I was nervous while I was waiting — but once I get rolling I'm fine."

"I can't even start."

"Well, I really wanted our team to win. All I thought about was knocking holes in the other side's arguments, and I guess I was listening so hard I forgot I was nervous. Besides, I'd read everything — " Vicky was eager to tell all she knew, but she could see she was talking too much. "Why? Do you have to give a speech?"

Lynn sat up. "I guess you could say that. The difference is, I don't want to make my speech but I have to."

"I'd help you practice."

Lynn tossed a chewing gum wrapper at Vicky. "Thanks, Vick. I don't think that will work. I've already practiced dozens of times."

"What you should do is belly-breathe. Nan says — " Vicky stopped again. Lynn did not want to hear it.

85

Lynn changed the subject. "Your mother won't make you get rid of them." Cleo twisted her head so that Lynn's fingers rubbed behind her ears. "They're too cute."

"You think your grandmother would take them if we had to?"

At the mention of her grandmother Lynn seemed flustered. "I don't know."

Lynn sat beside her Nikes, on the beach where Vicky said she would leave them. At the last minute she had decided to swim the half mile to shore. Vicky carried the sneakers in the boat with her.

No one else was on the beach. In the shadow of the trees Lynn stripped down to her underwear and wrung her T-shirt and shorts. She dressed again and laced her sneakers. That was better.

As she climbed the short stretch from the road, the car with the enormous tail fins was leaving Grammer's. It slowed, and the man and woman inside hailed Lynn as if they knew her. Lynn stared dumbly for a moment. She was so surprised all she could think was the guy needed a haircut. The overgrown car turned the corner onto Deerhill Road.

Grammer was sitting on the porch shelling peas. She slit a pod with her thumbnail and poured several into Lynn's hand.

"Who was that?" said Lynn.

"He calls himself Justin, he says, and she's Glory. They came to the back door and stuck their faces up to the screen. Scared me half to Portland. He asked if he could chop wood. I didn't have the heart to tell him I use Bob Reidy up the road. I thought they were some of them hippies. If they are, it's a new kind. They're not afraid of back-breaking work."

"You think they'll come back?"

"Poor as the parson's dog, from the looks of them. Mr. Davis and me started with more'n that."

"I said, do you think they'll come back? Are you going to give them work?"

"Oh. No. Probably not."

At feeding time Skip whistled from the guest house, while Vicky led the cats down the path, waving a warmed-over hamburger.

Nan protested. Couldn't they use something else? The cats got too excited over red meat. Vicky could end up scratched the way Skip did.

"Aww, Mom, they were jumpy because it was raw. This is how animal trainers train their animals. Dad found it in a book, when he took us to the library. After a while, we won't need meat. We just have to whistle."

"All right," said Nan. "If it keeps them out of the house."

Lynn ate little of her dinner. She toyed with the silver-ware and watched the minute hand on Grammer's stove clock push toward six. The glass face of the clock was scratched and blurred from years of cleanser. They put away the leftovers and washed the dishes. The minute hand continued its sweep.

Every day she had found reasons not to phone her parents. Excuses. It was the weekend and they would be out. Tuesday nights they both had meetings. It was too late to get that job in the camp, anyway. Or Grammer seemed like her old self. She could never quite make up her mind to call. She could hear her mother's I-told-you-so voice.

The hand pushed on to six-thirty. Both her parents would have arrived home by now. Lynn lifted the receiver. She hoped her father would answer. "Do you want me to reverse the charges?"

Grammer looked up from her gardening magazine. "You calling your folks?" Lynn nodded. "I see." Grammer paused. "To bring you home?"

Lynn nodded again, slower.

"Thought you forgot that business."

"I can't stay if you don't want me."

Grammer's brow furrowed. "I never said I stopped wanting you here. I don't want you nose-boxing me. That's a long difference."

Grammer turned Lynn from the phone and pressed her granddaughter to her soft bosom. She smelled warm, a little of clothes starch and perspiration, not the cloying sweet of other kids' grandmothers. "There are a lot of ways to look out for a person so's you don't insult them. That's what nose-boxing is — insulting."

Lynn was crying. "I won't do it again."

"I'm not used to being watched over, child. It's like a new suit of clothes. They're fighting me, binding in the elbows and the waist. Some day we'll bend at the same places."

12

❦❦❦

Long hours passed when Lynn did little more than watch the colors change on the barn or stare at drifting shadows of clouds. At home she had to pretend at least to be reading, and even then, her mother pumped her, crawling into her head until Lynn didn't know whether she thought the book was a waste because *she* felt that way, or because her mother did.

Here she knew where Grammer left off and where she began. Ever since they had cleared the air between them, Lynn could breathe again.

But, in spite of her resolve not to be a nose-box, Lynn felt herself tighten one day when she heard unfamiliar voices in the kitchen. From bits of conversation she knew it was the soup can people: "Justin, honey — " "Glory, you — " They had those funny names. So they had come back. Why on earth would Grammer let fruitcakes like them in?

Lynn walked into the kitchen as if Grammer often entertained unannounced company. "Hi," she said in an off-hand way. Her grandmother was nowhere to be seen. Lynn tried not to look too long or too obviously at them, but it was hard.

"Ayy, a fellow flat-footer!" the man crowed. He presented a stained, heavy-soled foot, along with a hand to slap five.

Lynn ignored the hand and drank her orange juice. Oh brother, would her mother have a coronary! "I wear shoes when I'm in school," said Lynn. She could feel herself blush. "Only I'm out right now."

"Whaddya know? Me too."

"Justin, pipe down. Can't you see you're scaring her? Your grandmother's outside, honey."

"I guess I'll go out and see what she's doing. Maybe I can help." Lynn backed into the screen door just as Grammer was entering. Grammer stooped to pick up the plant cuttings she dropped. "Oh. Sorry, Grammer." Lynn was so embarrassed she didn't know what else to do except continue on outside and sit on the back steps.

The brown-and-white dog was sniffing at shrubs and scuffing his back feet. Lynn's first impulse was to chase him away, but clearly he had come with his owners.

"Taste this," she heard Grammer say.

"It's stronger," marveled Glory.

"That's the peppermint. Try this."

"Wow!"

Grammer chuckled. "That'll grow your whiskers, son. Applemint. Ever heard of applemint? Makes a fine tea, too."

"Wow!" he said again.

Good grief, what a fake. Anyone who said "wow" that much had to be a fake. And the other one's pretended concern — "Can't you see you're scaring her?" Lynn leaned her head into the spicy-smelling blossoms climbing the trellis. Keeping her promise was not going to be easy.

* * *

"I think they're gone for good," said Skip.

"Good riddance," Vicky answered. Neither the soup can people, nor their dog, had been seen for days.

"Maybe we can leave the boat here afterward, then, instead of fastening the chain."

Vicky scowled. "If you'd put the key in the can, where it belongs, it wouldn't be such a big deal to find it."

Slowly Skip's face pursed into a hurt pucker. Fat tears dribbled and spilled onto the front of his shirt. He let go of his end of the boat. "You think I can't do anything right. Sometimes I wish I didn't know you."

"I'm older. I have to tell you," Vicky defended herself hotly.

"I hope I never get older, if I'm going to be like you."

Skip sat on his haunches next to the cats, who were sprawled in the sand. He picked at bits of twig in the soil, still weeping.

"Don't be a cry-baby. C'mon, Skip, will you? I thought you wanted to go to the island."

"Unh-uh."

No sooner did Skip refuse, than a yelping, howling animal hurled itself straight at the cats. The brown-and-white mongrel and the two cats collapsed into a snarling whorl of fur and teeth. The dog's jaw snapped for the scruff of Rudy's neck. Rudy somersaulted into the sand.

Skip was pushing into the center, trying to pry the animals apart. Vicky grabbed hold of a pantleg and jerked him backward. Skip bucked and kicked, digging his fingernails into the dirt. Several blows from his other leg connected with her side. Finally he was out of range of the fight.

She pinned his legs. "I hate you!" Skip shouted.

There were a few scratches on Skip's cheek, but mostly he was dirty, probably from being dragged across the ground. Vicky was so relieved she burst into tears. "You stupid idiot," she said, "I don't want you to get hurt."

Surprised, Skip stopped tossing.

She wiped her face. "Try calling the cats. I'll see if I can do something about the dog."

"Okay, Vick."

While Vicky yanked a sapling from among a mass of young trees, Skip ran toward the guest house. He whistled and called, but the cats were heedless. Vicky flailed her stick at the dog. The sapling could not do much more than sting, but maybe it would distract him.

By then the fight had attracted several on-lookers from the public beach, including the guy with the moped and his friends. "Hit him!" one of the boys chortled.

Vicky made a sour face. "I'm not trying to hurt him."

The dog turned to slash over his shoulder. Rudy and Cleo took advantage of the break and shot for a tree.

"Go, go!" Skip shouted.

The cats sprinted up the tree with the same agility they used to cover level ground, climbing to the topmost branches. Cleo went too far and careened on a slender limb, then backed down a few feet. She huddled in a notch next to Rudy, who watched the dog jumping and scratching below. Cleo exploded with a guttural that rose to a scream.

"The dog attacked first," Vicky said to a sunburned woman beside her.

"Yeah, he was trespassing," said Skip.

The dog had stopped jumping and lay in a heap, panting

heavily. A scrawny-chested man, carrying a beer can, pointed. "The mutt's cut up bad," he said. Already the flies and insects homed in on the blood-smeared coat. "Anybody know who owns him?"

"We do. I do," Vicky said, excited. "The people with the blue car — the big tail fins. There they are!" They were hurrying to the edge of the crowd. What was Lynn doing with them?

"Are the cats okay?" asked Lynn. "We could hear it all the way up to the house. I got them as fast as I could."

Glory was upset. "Billy," she said, starting toward the dog.

Justin put a hand out to restrain her. "He may bite."

"What'll we do?"

"Let me get my gloves. They're in the car." Justin rushed off.

Glory moved closer. "Here, Billy." The dog's tail thumped, but he made no effort to come to her. It was hard not to feel sorry for her, no matter what Lynn may have thought before.

"How about if I get some water?" said Skip.

"Oh yes. Thank you."

Skip brought Nan and Doug down with him. He filled the cats' bowl with fresh pond water and set it a few feet from the dog. "Here, Billy. Good Billy." The dog drew himself clumsily to his feet and padded to the water.

"Thank goodness," said Glory.

Doug touched her elbow sympathetically. "He'll be all right. Pups and children heal fast."

A woman with a baby gestured to the trees. "See the tigers? Pretty tigers," she cooed. Nan pulled Vicky and Skip close to her.

Howie laughed. "Those aren't tigers." He jabbed the yellow-haired boy next to him and whispered. "Easy eight hundred. Four hundred apiece. Maybe more," Lynn thought she heard him say. Their eyes fastened on the cats, the three boys buzzed in excited undertones.

Lynn shielded her eyes and stared up into the tree. They did look like tigers.

When Justin reappeared, he lifted the dog, grunting slightly. The dog yipped with pain and snapped at Justin's face, but Justin clamped a gloved hand around the dog's snout like a muzzle. "I've got to get him to a vet's," he said. "Anybody know where I can find one?"

Lynn spoke up. "My grandmother can tell you."

As soon as Grammer saw the dog, she ushered everyone into the kitchen. While she dug through her cabinets for cotton swabs and antiseptic, she ordered Lynn and Glory to lay out a clean sheet on the table and Justin to hold the dog.

Billy squirmed and whined at first, as Grammer checked him over. She patted the dog's rump. "Scared mostly. His nose and the scratch over his eye are nasty, but I don't find any bite wounds. It's the bite wounds that give the problems. I wager he won't rush to meet the next cat he sees." Grammer cleaned the cuts and in a short time Billy was resting more or less peacefully, while Grammer dickered with Justin about doing repairs on the barn.

Lynn listened from the living room. She wondered how long this Glory and Justin, and now Billy, were going to hang around. They never did get to a vet's.

Lynn knew what a moped cost new; halve that roughly for a used bike in good condition. "Easy eight hundred.

94

Four hundred apiece." Lynn assumed Howie meant dollars. Four hundred dollars could buy a second-hand moped, with some left over. Lynn had no doubt Howie's buddies wanted their own. She saw the way they cajoled constantly for a turn on his. Eight hundred would be two used mopeds, one for both Chris and Joe, and helmets. But why easy? Easy to get?

"Grammer?" They were on the porch again. Justin and Glory and the dog had driven off at last.

"Mm-mm?" she answered.

"If a kid around here wanted to make money, how would he do it?"

"Most of them go down to the resorts — wait table, that sort of thing — at Winnipesaukee."

"What about the younger kids?"

"Don't know about them. In your father's day the young ones collected bottles for the deposit."

"Can they trap animals to get money?"

"Certainly. Kids are putting out traps all the time. Homemade contraptions. That's not just the young ones. I tell 'em if anybody sets traps on my property it'll be me. Crazy kids. They'll drop traps anywhere and forget them. Hazel Reidy's terrier got himself stuck in one and they looked high and low for days. Poor dog nearly died."

Lynn came to attention. Maybe Howie was not lying. "What do they hunt?"

"Raccoons a lot of times. The kids here like to get themselves a raccoon and tame it. Take it fishing with them. I wouldn't advise it, though. One youngster over in Center Sandwich had to take the rabies shots. Terrible thing."

"They don't make any money that way."

95

"Sure they do. Sell the raccoons to tourists — a real boondoggle."

"Are they hard to catch?"

"All you need is garbage."

"Do they get a lot of money for a raccoon?"

"A lot of money? I've heard they go for twenty-five dollars on Winnipesaukee. Fifty dollars, if you bag a big tourist." Grammer snickered.

At twenty-five or fifty dollars a head, one moped, even used, was a lot of raccoons. And a lot of tourists to buy them. But Howie had said skins, not live animals. "What about selling animal skins — would you make a lot of money that way?"

Grammer squinted. "You planning to take up trapping?"

"No."

"You need money?"

Lynn giggled. "No."

"Well, before you rob the bank — " Grammer wagged a finger — "you want to trap your mink and your fox in winter, when the coat is heavy. You won't get rich on summer furs."

Lynn laughed again. The whole thing really was ridiculous. Howie and his friends were talking bikes, that was all. It didn't have anything to do with anything. An earthquake could go off under them and the only thing they would notice is they were missing a moped. Forget it, Lynn Davis.

The Seymours' VW station wagon was gone, and the barn doors unlocked. Lynn peeked in a window. She wanted to find out about the cats. She also wanted to explain to Vicky about the soup can people. Maybe they went for ice cream. She wished she had arrived earlier; a triple-dip soft chocolate with sprinkles would hit the spot.

Rudy and Cleo must be locked in the guest house. She could hear one of them. It was Cleo. Funny, how even animals had distinctive voices. "Hey, kitty, you're okay. Relax, Cleo."

She was about to try the guest house door, when she noticed the screen. It was ripped at the center, as if a rock or a fist had been heaved through it, and the paint was scraped. Someone had been jamming between the frame and the screen with a thin implement. There it was, practically at her feet. Lynn picked up a screwdriver. What would anybody want at the guest house?

13

❧❧❧

The Seymours weren't terribly concerned about the guest house when Lynn dropped by the next morning. Nan said the door had been like that when they came up, and no one else was sure one way or the other. Nan could be right; Doug wasn't much of a handyman and things always were waiting to be fixed.

Besides, Vicky and her mother were bickering over Skip, and from the tone of things it sounded like an argument about more than Skip, the way arguments about messy bedrooms were really over grades.

"Vick, let's end this," Nan said. "I know you're upset

about the cats, but look at how crazy they were to get out of the guest house this morning. How can we possibly confine them to an apartment all winter?"

Vicky moved her mother's hands away. "You can't get rid of the world's smartest cats like they're nothing."

"We'll talk tonight, when everyone is fed and calmed down. Now, please, stop making yourself miserable and stop trying to make me miserable." Nan hung up her apron and dishtowel and made it clear she was planning to work.

Vicky shot her mother an injured look and slammed out the screen door onto the porch.

"What's that all about?" said Lynn, trailing.

"Nan thinks Rudy and Cleo are too wild." Vicky discovered a balled-up sock in the chaise and threw it on the floor, indicating what she thought of that idea.

"Too wild to live in New York?"

"You got it." Vicky had found the mate to the first sock and threw it, too. "It's not fair. All Jimmy Porter's cat Snowball can do is sleep and eat, and once in a while, if he's not too tired, he purrs."

"Are Rudy and Cleo okay?"

"Rudy was limping a little, but he's better this morning. They didn't really get hurt. Dumb dog. My mother wouldn't be so hot to get rid of the cats if it weren't for him." But Vicky knew that was only half true. The fight with the dog was merely the last in a chain of incidents. "Who are those creeps, anyway?"

Lynn suppressed an apologetic "I don't know." "My grandmother hired them to do some odd jobs."

"Oh great. So we can have a few more cat and dog fights."

"Grammer doesn't think the dog will bother them again. She says he's learned his lesson."

"Better have."

Lynn wanted to see the cats for herself, but they were with Skip. They found him on the beach, showing Howie the way Cleo and Rudy could swim.

"Man, that's great," said Howie, as Cleo stepped out of the water with the wet ball clenched between her teeth. "Let me try," he said, leaning over for the sponge, but Cleo growled and backed away from Howie's outstretched fingers.

"You have to let her drop it first," said Skip. "Otherwise, she gets mad."

Howie grinned. "Oh yeah? A real fighter. She scratch and stuff?"

"Yeah," said Skip with a tinge of pride, even though he knew Howie was goading him.

Howie noticed Lynn and Vicky. "I've never seen cats swim like that," he commented. "How did you get them to do it?" Vicky explained.

Howie seemed to lose interest in the cats suddenly. He offered Skip a ride on his moped. Skip's eyes widened into saucers. "Oh, brother — would I!" After they made several loops around the parking lot, Howie let Skip try pedaling to start it, and later they fashioned a kind of zigzag race course, using soda cans. They talked for a long time out of earshot of the two girls, with Skip obviously asking a lot of questions, and Howie showing him various features of the bike.

When it came to his ped Howie wasn't nearly this good to Chris and Joe, Lynn noted. Skip was so much younger and clearly in awe of him. Howie probably was your basic

99

decent guy. She didn't know why she was always so negative about him.

"When I get a ped, I'm going to drill out my tailpipe like Howie's," said Skip, still glowing, as they trudged the hill to the cottage.

"What does that do?" asked Lynn.

"Makes it go faster."

"Too bad we can't do the same with your head — make it go faster," Vicky needled.

"Lay off," Skip grumbled. "All you care is how smart people are. You think smart is the junk you know. Howie's smart. He can tell me all about mopeds and how to fix them. You can't."

"Who cares about mopeds? I don't want to know any of that."

"And I don't want to know what you know. So we're even." Skip ran ahead on the path.

"For crying out loud. I was only joking," Vicky called.

Skip was shuffling the cards for a game of Knock Rummy. Lynn sat in for Nan, while she fixed popcorn. Doug thumped the table. "Redeal. Dealer peeked at the cards."

"Aww, cut it out, Dad."

"This is a gaming table. I want a little mirth."

"How can anybody be happy around here," Vicky grumped, "when we have Dr. and Mrs. No for parents."

"Very clever, dah-link," said Doug, doing a passable imitation of a Hungarian movie star, "but not funny. You've been reading that spy stuff again."

"Come on, Dad, why can't we bring them back to New

100

York?" There was no point in asking her mother, but Doug was wavering.

"Talk to Nan, not me," he said.

"Chicken."

Nan jumped in. "Because we agreed. Rudy and Cleo are not ordinary cats. You agreed, Vick. Skip agrees. Your father agrees. They are too wild to be confined to a six-room apartment."

"Then I'm not going back. I'm staying with the cats," said Skip. "For always."

Nan banged the bowl of popcorn so hard the top layer scattered over the table. She glared at her son, eyeball to eyeball. "Over my dead body."

Doug ahemed, winking at Lynn. "I thought we were going to discuss alternatives." He did a drumroll on the edge of the table. "Pah-pah-pah-pah. Al-ter-na-tives. Al-ter-na-tives."

Lynn laughed. She loved sitting in on the Seymours' discussions. People got mad and yelled and then out of the blue they would all be joking.

"Let's be organized about this," said Doug, playing another drumroll. "Lynn Davis is appointed recording secretary. Everyone agreed?"

"I need paper and pencil," said Lynn.

"Done." Doug flipped over the score sheet and handed it to Lynn. "Now, Mother, I know you aren't going to like this," Doug said, holding up a hand to ward off displeasure, "but taking the cats home with us is one alternative."

"One," Nan conceded. She had calmed down and pulled up a chair. "We also have plenty of time to find them a good home here. That's one alternative. Or we might simply release them."

"Release them how?"

"Let them go it on their own. They'll hunt their own food, live out-of-doors. They're practically doing it now." One or the other of the cats was always dropping a mole or a frightened mouse at their feet.

Skip asked, "You mean like wild animals? I saw on TV once how these people taught these birds — big ones, like eagles — how to live out on cliffs. We could teach Rudy and Cleo to live in the woods and not to go to humans for food." Then he thought better of it. "Except us. They'd still be ours, Vick. We could make a movie — like the guys with the birds."

"Hold it," said Doug. "There's a chance the cats might not show up again, Skip. And you'd never know why."

"Not if we left them on the island," said Vicky. "They'd be there when we came back next summer."

"Not enough food to hold them over a winter, Vick."

"We'll catch a lot of mice and leave them on the island, too!" Skip exclaimed.

Doug chuckled. "Can you see us ferrying zillions of mice across in the canoe?" He tweaked Skip's nose. "Orville Alva Einstein, it just might work. Okay, that's one plan. What about giving them to someone? Who can we give them to? Lynn, you want a couple of cats?"

"My mother would kill me."

"Your grandmother?" said Nan.

"She might."

"Howie," said Skip. "He wanted to know what we were going to do with Rudy and Cleo. He sounded like he'd like to have them." Lynn wrote Howie's name on her list after her grandmother's.

Vicky had been thinking. "Maybe there's a way to make the cats not so wild."

"You mean de-claw them?"

"No, not that. See, Lynn says good riding horses have to be trained to a bridle and saddle. They don't automatically let you hop on their backs. Am I right?" Lynn agreed. "Maybe it's the same with cats," said Vicky. "Some cats make good housecats because they don't know anything different, but Rudy and Cleo have to learn how."

Skip's face brightened. "We'll civilian-ize them."

"Civil-ize them," Nan corrected. "I'm not convinced that can be done."

"You could let us try," Vicky begged. "One chance."

"Vick, there's something different about these cats. I don't think — "

"We want to try one chance," parroted Skip.

Nan's forehead sank to rest on her hand. "Oh, my curtains."

"I think that was a concession statement, kids," said Doug.

"Y-a-ay!"

"The recording secretary will now read the report — "

"Wait," Nan interrupted. "I do not concede until we have agreed on criteria."

"Mutually-acceptable-standards-for-the-achievement-of cat-civilization. Okay, group, how will Mom know it's safe to take the cats home with us?"

"We'll teach them not to scratch the furniture," piped up Skip.

"Or to climb curtains," Doug coached. "You better stick that one in."

"If we could train the cats to a leash, to heel, and all that jazz, would you accept that as proof?" Vicky proposed.

"All right!" Doug cheered. "That's got to be the ultimate in cat civilization."

Nan looked at the circle of expectant faces. "Why am I always the bad guy?" she lamented. "Yes, that sounds more than fair, if — "

"If?" said Doug. "Let this be a lesson to you, cat-training fans. Watch those if's, and's, and but's. Here comes the kicker."

"Doug, stop," Nan protested. "I was only going to say — if they are also trained to a litter box."

Everyone laughed. "You've got to admit, cat trainers, your mother thinks of everything."

Later that evening Lynn and Vicky and Skip sat on the beach, watching leftover Fourth of July sparklers spit and fizz at the dark. Winning another chance for Cleo and Rudy seemed good cause for celebration. Vicky was full of visions of the cats trotting proudly at the end of a leash onto the Staten Island Ferry, or grooming themselves beside the library's stone lions. Nan was going to be stunned at how well-behaved they could be, good enough to live among people and high-rise apartments and elevators.

Then they heard the moped and saw a long shaft of light fanning out over the water. "Hey, it's Howie," said Skip. "Hey, Howie," he cried, scrambling to his feet and racing to the service road. A short while later Skip returned, dragging his heels.

"What's up, Skipper?" asked Lynn.

"Nothing."

"Howie wouldn't give you a ride?"

"Nah. He says he's going night fishing."

"Too bad." Night fishing. Did people go night fishing? wondered Lynn. Or more important, did Howie go night fishing?

14

❧❧❧

Justin lifted aside the tent flap. "Madam. Ladies. Sir Charles." He bowed to Grammer, to Vicky and Lynn, then Skip. "Home sweet home."

The tent was so cramped once everyone was seated inside that Justin's legs stuck though the opening. "If we bend the knees — like this — and — zip — zip — zip — like so," he said, drawing a nylon tab, "we have air, and no creepy-crawlies. And — for privacy, we use this one." He pulled another tab and a second flap covered the opening, sealing them in a blue dome. It was like putting on tinted glasses.

"How on earth do you sleep in here?" said Grammer. "My backside is stiff already."

Justin reached behind a sleeping bag and produced a thin piece of foam rubber tied jelly-roll fashion. He patted. "This is the magic carpet."

Grammer squeezed the mat. "Have to be a lot of magic to sleep on that."

"How are you doing?" Glory's voice called from outside.

"Away. Away. No room."

"Yes there is."

Justin sighed. He opened the flap once more and Glory crawled in beside him, with Skip curling in Justin's lap to make room. Justin pretended to scowl. "Madam," he addressed Grammer in butler-like tones, "may I get you anything? A lemonade? An overstuffed chair? Yes? I happen to have the perfect item." He reached again into the gear piled at the edges of the tent.

"Justin, what's that?"

"Wait." Justin lifted Skip into Glory's lap, then placed a folded plastic thing to his lips and blew. After a while the green plastic was crinkling noisily.

"It's a giant potato chip bag," guessed Vicky.

"Nope." Justin continued to blow. The thing was spreading and taking up so much space that Glory crawled out the front flap. Soon everyone left, except Justin, who puffed, mopped his brow, puffed and mopped. At long last the hissing monster unfolded. Justin paused to admire the result. "Wow! All that air was in me."

"Jus?"

"Patience." He licked the plug, sealed it carefully, and rotated the monster on its side.

"You actually bought it? I thought you were kidding," said Glory.

Lynn squealed. "Grammer, it's a chair!"

Suddenly Glory was laughing uncontrollably. "You blew yourself in."

There was no disputing it. Justin was imprisoned behind the chair. "I know one way to fix that," he said.

"Hear, hear, young fella. Before you go wasting precious hot air, I'm going to set in it." Grammer stooped. "Am I pointed right?" she said, backing into the tent. "Tell me when." "Now," said Justin, and Grammer let herself drop. The seat was so bouncy she sat doubled over to avoid bursting through the top of the tent. "Mighty fine chair," she remarked. "I'd say near perfect for cleaning between your toes."

Justin plumped the rear with his feet. "Careful! I control the plug."

After they shared a lunch of sprouts and pita bread, which Grammer said must be healthy, because it surely didn't have taste, the six of them tied the inflated chair to the roof of Justin's car and drove — slowly — to Deerhill.

Down at the pond, Justin tried to use the monster chair as a float, but as soon as he took his feet off the bottom, he rolled over. He tried jumping into it and paddling furiously with his hands. He tried deflating it slightly, thinking it rode too high in the water. He tried adding more weight by taking on Skip as a passenger, but no matter what he did, he could not keep the monster from tipping. Finally he flopped, stomach first, onto its backside. "Go La-Z-Boy!" he hollered, bobbing above the water line.

Lynn had laughed so much her sides still ached when she got up the next morning and sipped her cocoa on the porch.

It was strange how much her feelings about Glory and Justin had changed. People could seem to be one thing, then something so completely different when you knew them up close. When Glory and Justin were the soup can people, she had resented their dropping by, morning or evening, with hardly an excuse. Sometimes they had stayed only long enough to say hello. Sometimes they worked — candling eggs, whitewashing the chicken coop, stringing green beans to dry. Glory weeded. Justin oiled hinges and pounded nails in floorboards that had been loose so long Lynn missed their complaining noises.

Over time Billy learned to keep his distance from the Seymours' cats. And somehow Glory and Justin had ceased to be the soup can people — perhaps because they were so much themselves. Now if they dropped by the farm and Lynn hung around, it was because she wanted to be with them, not because she felt she had to keep a suspicious eye on things.

Justin and Glory might be weird, but it was a "fun" weird.

"What do you think of where they're staying?" Grammer asked.

So she was thinking about them, too. "The campgrounds? They're okay. Kind of crowded."

"Too close to Boston. Pretty near every college kid can lay his hands on a tent and a sleeping bag. What if I offer them a place to camp? They more than paid the rent, what with the work they've done. Besides," snorted Grammer, "they need more room now with that chair contraption."

"I'd like that," Lynn answered.

Grammer was silent awhile, her rocker scratching its familiar tune on the porch. "Not like me to favor strangers. Half the time I don't favor people I know. Reminded me of Mr. Davis, the boy did, soon as he opened his mouth. A gosh-aw-golly gee-whizzer like your Grandfather Davis, tickling every bit of enjoyment out of a thing. Mr. Davis didn't look as peculiar, but he was different, just the same. Never out of spite, though. I'm the kind that's butting people with my horns to run the other direction, because I can't tolerate being herded. His running was like a kid that recently learned how. People like him and Mr. Davis — they're the free ones."

Skip had abandoned their project early in the day, so while Vicky persisted single-handedly, he was collecting rocks to wing across the water. Vicky snatched a stone from him and hurled it into the trees. "How many times do I have to tell you? Smooth, flat stones work the best."

"I like it when they flop."

"Your problem, Skip, is you're mediocre, and it's only us perfectionists who will ever get it right." Vicky turned back to the cats. "Hear that?" she complained at them. "I'll make you do it, if it takes me forever."

"I think the leash is tight," said Skip.

Vicky thought briefly about dumping her brother on a cliff with a certain two cats so he could have his wish to be in the movies. "That's the idea. If it's loose, they get out, nitwit."

The program to civilize the cats was floundering: The cats had spurned the litter box. As for training them to a leash, in a collar of any sort, Rudy and Cleo simply hunched, wiggled, and backed away from the straps until the noose slid over their heads.

With Nan's help Vicky had devised a figure-eight harness out of clothesline. When the cats understood there was no escaping the leash they rolled over and lay on their sides, and as long as it was on, nothing would force them to stand, let alone to move.

Finally Vicky left them tied to a pole, figuring they would have to get up sometime. After a couple of hours they did. Overjoyed, she took the cats for a walk, which lasted as far as the daylilies. One tug on the rope and they went limp.

July had vanished. August was wasting away. They hadn't begun curtain and furniture training yet. How would they ever make it to the ninth floor of an apartment building? Vicky could see the cats now, backing away from a crowded elevator, refusing to enter. Elevator after elevator slammed shut, leaving them stranded on the ground floor.

"Come on, Cleo, you creep. Up!"

Nan was watching from the kitchen window. "Don't torture yourself, Vick. Enjoy them. September will be here before you know it."

No sooner had Grammer mentioned her offer to Justin and Glory than they were hopping into the car with promises to return. "Good thing once my mind is made up it stays put," Grammer said to Lynn. She was alternately grinning and whistling off key. "I wouldn't have had a chance to change it."

Grammer suggested Glory and Justin pitch their tent in the meadow. "You'll not have to look at us any more than you want, and there's running water nearby in the barn." But Lynn lobbied for the cove. It was scenic, certainly better for building campfires. "Yes, I suppose," Grammer conceded. For a moment she sounded so sad.

Lynn showed Glory and Justin the shortcut. She was impatient for them to admire the site, but they were weighed down with camping gear. Justin dropped the tent, which was folded into a remarkably compact package, and he and Glory helped each other slide from under their backpacks. At last Justin paced the length and width of the beach. He swung through a full circle. "It sure beats lining up alongside two dozen other scouts," he said. "We'll take it."

"Hallelujah!" Glory shouted and planted a kiss on Justin.

They decided to erect the tent in a small clearing a short distance from the beach where it would be protected by tree branches. "Better than an air-conditioner," said Glory, "and we can still see the water."

That settled, Lynn went to the Seymours' to recruit help cleaning up the cove area. Vicky was grateful for an excuse to let the cats off their leashes.

"How's it going?"

"Bad," Vicky answered.

"Look at that," she said, as they walked along the shoreline, the cats tagging close behind. "Without their leashes, they'll come with me. Put them on and bingo — they've got four broken legs."

"Maybe you should forget about the leash and concentrate on the rest."

"I'm sorry I dreamed it up, but now Nan thinks it's a good idea. 'The cats should be under control,' she says. 'There are lots of frightening sounds in New York.' Sometimes I think the cats really understand and they won't learn how, on purpose." Vicky looked down at the animals and scolded. "You're like Skip. Stubborn."

With many hands pitching in, the tent practically put itself up, just as Justin and Glory promised. They hauled away the beach litter — mostly the remains of a bonfire — stacked fallen branches for firewood, and took turns at inflating Grammer's chair.

Rudy and Cleo promptly claimed the tent for themselves. Seated in the opening, they looked like master and
mistress of the house, grooming, pausing occasionally to
heed a passing sound or bird.

Everything was ready for Grammer to inspect. They
brought her down on Smoke, despite her protests that it
was pure nosiness to barge in on guests so soon.

Coming into the cove, Lynn could see Grammer's jaw
clench. She let Smoke slow to a standstill, wondering what
was worrying her. "Goodness, move this horse along,
child," Grammer commanded. "I'm not that much in fear
of falling." Lynn looked up. Had she imagined it?

After a cursory tour of the campsite, Grammer made a
few admiring comments, then asked to leave.

Justin was disappointed. "You just came. Here, sit in
your chair."

"Young man, I'm too old to be making this fool trip.
From now on, you want to be neighborly, you come to the
house."

"Too old?" Justin sputtered. "Since when — ?" But
Grammer was not listening.

Glory took Justin's arm to quiet him. "Leave her alone,
Jus. Can't you see something's upset her?"

15

✿✿✿

At night Vicky often made up stories for her brother. Skip's favorite was that Justin was the son of the King of the Gypsies, banished and forced to wander in a broken-down car. Vicky had read once the King lived in Philadelphia — or was it New York? Anyway, he was real, but the rest of it was fantasy.

She never dreamed Skip would come right out and ask Justin. When Skip spilled the beans, Justin acted as if it were the most natural thing in the world for someone to think he was a Gypsy. He jammed his fists in his pockets and said, "I hope we haven't been deceiving you. We didn't intend to. Did we, Glory?"

Glory was sitting beside the cold campfire, her arms wrapped around her legs, with Lynn across from her. She shook her head gravely. "We sure didn't."

"Well, are you or aren't you?"

"My father drives a dry cleaning truck. He's driven his route since I was a kid."

"What a bummer," said Skip. In a strange way Vicky felt cheated, too.

"We only live like this summers," Justin said, motioning to the tent. "The rest of the year we live with Glory's parents. Glory and I are schoolteachers out in Illinois. She teaches kindergarten and I teach fourth."

"How come you didn't tell us?" Skip demanded.

"It never came up."

Justin looked Skip square in the face. "Ayy, little buddy, it was important to you that Glory and I be free and easy, wasn't it? Sleeping in tents and driving a rusty car. You figured those are the kind of people who live right. Outdoors. No responsibility. Only good times. Right?" Skip nodded. "I wish I knew people like that, too."

Justin chucked Skip's chin. "A lot of the kids who get me for a teacher feel the same way. Tell you what," he said. "Let's take a walk on over to the blueberry bushes. Maybe I can convince you I'm not such a bad guy. Not a prince, but not bad."

Skip and Justin strolled off with Billy on a leash. Billy made it look simple, thought Vicky.

Glory was carrying sleeping bags from the tent. The two girls helped spread the unzipped bags on bushes, exposing the linings to the sun to freshen them.

"Why do you bum around, if you don't have to?" said Vicky.

Glory smiled. "That's the way it must look." She searched for an answer. "Do you remember when you were little," she asked Vicky, "and you used to think your teacher lived at the school? And if you ever saw her at the grocery store you both were embarrassed?"

"That's dumb," said Vicky.

But Lynn understood. "I saw my second-grade teacher once at a restaurant. I nearly died trying to walk past her table." She laughed.

"No?" Glory asked Vicky again, looking for some glimmer of recognition. "Maybe it only happens in small towns. You go to the dentist, you see one of your kids. You go to a fast-food place, you see one of your kids. I have to hide the junk food in the bottom of my grocery cart," Glory joked, "so I don't disappoint somebody's mother." She sighed. "Somebody is always expecting you to set an example."

"So you travel," said Lynn.

"More than travel," said Glory. "We're different people. June comes, the schools close, we poke a spot on the map and work our way there. Justin throws his shoes in the back of the car and grows a beard. I forget to shave my legs. We buy clothes at not-new shops, and half the time we eat out of cans by the side of the road.

"When we're low on money, we hire out, doing repairs, cleaning. I waitress, which is interesting for a while — the people you meet — but it doesn't appeal to my feet much, so I quit as soon as I can."

"Don't you start to feel — I don't know — scummy?"

"Oh sure. We're always looking for a clean john to wash up," said Glory. "By the end of summer we're ready to go back — regular people with regular routines. But some day we'll find the place we belong, for keeps."

As they hiked to Grammer's shed for water, Glory continued. "See, Justin had this bachelor uncle who used to disappear every once in a while in his pickup to prospect in Michigan and West Virginia — that's how we got started. Wildcatting, he called it. Usually he said he was looking for oil, but we all knew better."

"Did he ever find anything?"

"No. No oil, or gold, no iron ore. Only a little coal. He

came home poorer than when he left, but it was dollars and cents poor, if you know what I mean. To hear him talk, he always struck it rich. He must have made dozens of these trips."

This uncle of Justin's sounded a little cuckoo.

"Where have you been?" asked Lynn.

"All over. The first summer Justin's thumb landed on Texas. We drove through two second-hand cars." Glory grinned. "That's why Justin's such a whiz on carburetors now. This year we were heading for Maine. We got as far as Boston and we met a psychiatrist and her husband at one of those outdoor concerts and we got to talking. You know how Justin is.

"They convinced us to house-sit for them. They went to California for a convention. Then they were taking their kids to the San Diego Zoo." Glory's eyes rolled. "It was a plantation, practically. A tennis court in back and a computer in the kids' playroom. Two dishwashers. Can you believe it?"

Lynn and Vicky exchanged glances. They could believe it.

"They had this complicated alarm system on all the doors and windows and you had to lock them in so many seconds or the bells went off and the police came. I couldn't get the hang of it. Every time I let in their dog, or Billy, a police car drove up." Glory giggled.

"At first everything was a knockout. Justin and I'd keep finding things. Wow this. Wow that. Like the house was a museum. But after a while you can't react.

"Their dog was a honey, though. A big, sweet mutt, like Justin. With this long blue-black fur. And overfed, like his house. He was so homely, then other times you'd look and he was gorgeous. I carded some of his fur and tried spinning it into yarn."

"Dog fur into yarn?" said Vicky.

"It wouldn't make a pair of mittens, but my kindergartners will get a kick out of it. You want to see it?"

They followed her to the car. "Did you ever get to Maine?" Vicky asked.

"No, the people we were house-sitting for told us about this place, so we drove here. The biggest mountain we have in Illinois is the ramp over the turnpike."

The hinges squealed as Glory lifted the lid to the trunk. The rear end was crammed with clothing, flats of canned peaches, canned corn, canned soups, and canned tuna, a guitar case, a gasoline can, laundry soap, a brown grocery bag of tools, even a cinder block.

"What's this?" said Vicky, pointing out the cinder block.

"That? Sometimes the emergency brakes don't work too well. Jus puts it behind a tire when we're parked. Then the car won't roll backwards."

Her mother would have started a headache on the spot, thought Lynn.

"Glory?"

Glory was pushing things aside to reach deeper into the trunk. "Hm?" She looked over her shoulder at Lynn.

"You're not looking for oil or anything, are you?"

Glory did not answer. She passed a ball of yarn to Lynn. Lynn squeezed. It was coarse and spongy. Glory took it back from Lynn and held it against the sky. As her hand turned, the bristly yarn glittered with sun-snatched color, now blue-black, now purple, then fiery gold. "This is what I'm wildcatting. Things like this. Things I didn't know at first were there."

"Look what we found," Justin announced when he and Skip came back to camp.

"It's a box," said Lynn, wondering why the excitement.

"But look here." Justin plucked a small wooden pin. "The slightest pressure on this wire trips the pin, and down comes this sliding door." He drew something from his pocket. "Smell."

Lynn and Vicky sniffed the pouch. Neither of them knew what it was.

"Catnip," said Glory, after she took a whiff.

"The catnip is attached to the wire. Some animal moseys in, bats the catnip with a paw, and he's trapped inside. It's a clever little device."

Skip could contain himself no longer. "I told you that was a trap!"

"What was?" said Vicky, bewildered.

"The box near the guest house."

"You mean that stinky thing I keep tripping over?"

"It's a trap," Skip insisted.

"Where did you find this?" Glory asked.

"On the shortcut from the logging trail to our path," said Skip. "I was showing Justin the cave."

"Oh, yeah," Vicky remembered. "Nan made us stop playing there, because she was afraid we might knock one of the dead trees loose and the whole works would come down."

Glory looked to Justin. "Why would anyone go to all this trouble to catch a cat? Or can you catch other things with catnip?"

"That's what I've been trying to figure out," he said. "Unless maybe someone lost a cat."

Vicky's heart leapt. "What if it's Rudy and Cleo's mother?"

"And if it's not a lost cat —?" said Glory.

"Then they're hunting at the wrong time of year. Usually people trap in the winter."

"Raccoons," suggested Lynn. "They have their babies in the spring. My grandmother says kids around here sell them for pets."

"Catnip to catch a raccoon?" Justin frowned. Lynn had to admit it made little sense.

"Oh, goody — a mystery!" said Skip.

Justin crouched beside him. "Ahh, but what's mystery without curiosity? One sees a thing and wonders why. Shazaam! — a mystery." His laugh exploded as he clapped Skip on the back. "Okay, pal, let me look at this other trap you were telling me about."

Glory and Lynn were grooming Smoke the next day when Vicky came rushing to the barn, out of breath and frightened. "Cleo," she panted. "She didn't come back last night for her dinner. And she didn't come this morning. You've got to help me find her."

"Slow down," said Glory. "What makes you think she needs to be found? Cats love to roam."

"Because they hate me. I've been making them drag around all time with those stupid leashes on. They won't even come to me anymore. They only go to Skip. Cleo's run away — I know it."

"Did you check the tent?" said Lynn.

"She's probably down there now," said Glory.

"No, no." Vicky would not be reassured. "I've looked in the tent at least a hundred times. Lynn, please. She might come to you. She knows you."

Vicky wasn't kidding. "Okay," said Lynn, "where do you want me to look?"

There were lots of small ravines off the trails where boulders had been discarded or low-lying fences were built with smaller rocks. Any of them would be large enough to conceal a cat. Vicky and Lynn tramped all day, reporting back to the cottage every so often in case Cleo had reappeared. Finally Nan insisted they stop for supper. Vicky would have continued searching and calling, but Lynn was glad for the chance to rest her throat and aching feet.

The only thing that turned up was another trap — this one clearly store-bought — made of wire with a spring-loaded door and a catnip pouch tied to it.

Lynn had come across it first in a ravine below Howie's mudhole where Smoke was frightened off the trail. She looked up to the ridge. The cage would have been easy enough to miss. Was it there that day? She released the spring and covered over the trap with debris before Vicky reached her.

When Lynn arrived home, Grammer was on the front porch, dozing over her photo album. Lynn tipped the rocker gently. "Grammer," she coaxed her awake, "I need to talk to you."

Grammer looked baffled at first, then she smiled and stretched. "Didn't know where I was."

"Sorry, Grammer, but it may be important." Lynn plunged into her questions. "Why would anyone leave catnip in a trap? What are they trying to catch?"

Grammer raised an eyebrow. She yawned. "Cats."

"Anything else?"

"Cats." Grammer said it louder the second time.

"What kind of cats?"

"All kinds. They all love catnip. Never knew a cat that didn't." Grammer yawned again.

"Cleo's missing. I think someone may want to kill her."

"That doesn't surprise me at all." Grammer got up from her chair and wobbled across the porch and down the steps, brushing aside Lynn's attempts to help. "When the chickens are all's left," she grumbled, "you can't have bobs sneaking about."

"Why would anyone want to kill her?" Lynn pursued.

"What do you think they've got there, child? Those aren't your ordinary, lap-sitting critters. Those are cunning, thieving wildcats. Bobs we called them. Nobody in his right mind takes in a bobcat, not on a farm. I wouldn't have a chicken left inside of a week." She stabbed at Lynn with her finger. "I'd make a no-account farmer if I didn't know you can't tame a bob."

"Someone would kill her to keep her away from chickens?"

"Leave me be, child. You're spoiling my dreams," and Grammer headed off toward the potting shed.

It wasn't Grammer's pills, Lynn thought. She had taken them first thing before breakfast. Lynn went to bring Grammer back to the house. The last thing she needed was to have her wandering around in the dark.

Later, Lynn slipped out and found the album on the

porch. She could remember the picture: Grandfather Davis and Grammer, a baby, and the two cats. There it was. Lynn held the picture in the beam of her flashlight. She would swear those cats looked exactly like Rudy and Cleo, a little larger, perhaps. She studied the picture, memorizing every detail before she tucked it into the white corners, and replaced the album on the floor beside the rocker.

If Rudy and Cleo were bobcats, the animals in the picture must be, too. No farmer would keep bobcats, yet her grandmother once had a pair. It did not make sense.

Some things, though, were falling into place. She remembered back over the times Grammer acted strangely. One way or another they were connected to the Seymours' cats.

16

❧❧❧

All evening Grammer had seemed bewildered, as if she were in two places at once and did not know which events belonged where. Lynn was afraid to leave her alone, but what she had to tell Vicky would not wait.

She tiptoed inside and dialed the phone. The clicking was so loud; she worried Grammer might overhear her talking. "Vick?" she said softly. Vicky sounded unhappy. This won't make her any happier, thought Lynn. "Cleo didn't run away."

"How do you know?"

"Remember how we always wondered what happened to the mother cat?"

"Sure."

"Grammer says Rudy and Cleo are bobcats. That means the mother was, too."

"Bobcats? But those are wild animals." Vicky was quiet a moment. "No wonder." The stubby tail, the heads that were starting to look so boxy, the tufts on their ears. Skip had tried to tell her they didn't look like regular cats. And the way they were so ferocious around raw meat. "I can't believe we didn't figure it out," said Vicky. "We knew they were wild, but not that wild."

"I think whoever's putting out those traps caught the mother. And maybe has Cleo."

"What for?"

Lynn was seized suddenly with caution. She was not certain enough of her suspicions to voice them. What if it was only a stupid story Howie told to impress her? "I guess they can be pretty bad — stealing chickens and all that stuff."

"Wait a minute. How does your grandmother know?" Vicky was not ready to have everything turned upside down so easily.

"Because she knows a lot about animals. What are you going to do now?" said Lynn.

"Keep looking, I guess. Find out who has chickens." Vicky hesitated. "What about your grandmother?"

"Come on, Vick," Lynn snapped. The silence that followed was so heavy it would have sunk even Justin's monster chair. Lynn cleared her throat. "My grandmother couldn't lug a trap with a live animal in it through the woods."

"I'm sorry. It was a stupid thing to say."

"Let's forget it."

"Do you know the names of the people on the road? I could call them tonight."

"Some. My grandmother's asleep. I can get the rest in the morning."

"Never mind. I don't want to wait that long. I'll get a flashlight and look on their mailboxes."

True to form, Vicky did not bother phoning either. She simply knocked at each door and asked her question in person.

A few hours later she was describing her visits up and down Deerhill Road to Lynn. "I asked them if they had chickens, and if they said no, I said good-bye and left." Vicky giggled so hard the tears rolled down her cheeks. They both were getting punch-drunk; it was late and they were tired. Vicky was going to sleep over.

"Shh," Lynn warned, nodding toward Grammer's door.

"Anyway," whispered Vicky, "no one right around here is trapping bobcats. So it has to be someone from farther away, which is kind of dumb."

"What do you mean?"

"The cats aren't any threat to chickens far away. That old Mrs. Reidy — the lady that sells the honey? — she said bobcats didn't usually poach except in the winter or in a drought year, when it was hard to find food."

"She knew about them?"

"She sounded like she did. She said there used to be lots and lots of them. Hey, I'm going into Laconia tomorrow with my dad. You want to come?"

"What are you going to do there?"

"Go to the library and find out everything I can about

bobcats. It can't be any more useless than walking around in circles in the woods." Vicky stretched out on her sleeping bag. "I don't get it. If you wanted to protect your chickens, you'd put traps on your own property, wouldn't you? or near it? Why put them by the pond?"

The next day Cleo still was missing: two nights in a row. Poor Rudy. Skip would not let him out of his sight.

"If she comes back, lock her in the guest house," Vicky ordered.

"No, the barn," said Lynn, remembering the broken screen.

At the library they started with the periodicals, which Doug said was the best way to get a lot of information quickly. After a while he returned from his errands and helped them read. "Somebody beat us to it." He pushed an article at Vicky. Facing the story was a full-page picture of a young bobcat in water, wet fur molded to his head, the chin thrust forward, the same way Rudy and Cleo looked swimming.

Lynn leafed through the next magazine and found another article. This one reported a booming market in domestic cat furs. All the others she read had talked about bobcat lore and eating and breeding habits. Lynn gazed at the ceiling.

Of course. She remembered one of her mother's friends winning a lynx coat as a door prize at some benefit auction or other. *Lynx rufus,* there it was, the Latin name for the bobcat. Lynn flipped to the cover to check the date. Less than a year old.

Then a phrase leapt from the glossy page: "up to four hundred dollars a pelt." Howie's "easy four hundred"! She bet that would buy more than a used moped and a helmet. It probably would buy a fancy wire cage, too — for trapping more easy money.

Lynn hid the tremor in her hand as she passed the article to Vicky in exchange for a magazine from her pile. Vicky's magazine was opened to a picture of a man with a gun in a rakish pose beside forty or fifty pelts drying on a fence.

During the drive home, Doug's quips and anecdotes were falling flat. Vicky finally squelched him. "Dad, can the humor."

"Sorry, I thought maybe we could use a little. It doesn't look good, library fans. Those traps are not sitting out there to do any good."

"No kidding," Vicky retorted. "How could anybody do anything as gross as that? Turn Cleo into a fur coat. It's gross, gross, gross!" She pounded the dashboard.

Lynn, who had been quiet most of the trip, spoke up. "I know how. For the money." Her suspicions about Howie tumbled out at last.

"Can we do anything, Dad?" Vicky asked when Lynn was finished.

Doug was thoughtful. "Legal action? I doubt it."

"What about leaving traps on other people's property? We have some rights. They're trespassing."

"Okay, good point. I'll make a few calls when we get home. See what we can find out about this."

As soon as they pulled into the driveway, Skip bounded to the station wagon. He looked so happy Vicky was convinced Cleo had returned.

"Howie's helping me look for Cleo," Skip announced proudly.

"You dodo!" Vicky screamed.

Skip was crushed. "You said you weren't going to call me names."

"If you'd smarten up, it wouldn't be so hard to remember."

"We think someone is putting out those traps to catch Rudy and Cleo," Lynn tried to explain.

"What for?"

"Probably to make coats."

"Cat fur coats?"

"They do it to rabbits, don't they?" said Vicky.

"Do they — You think they kill them?"

"That's what this is all about, dum — " Vicky stopped herself in time. "How else do you think they get the fur?"

"Maybe like sheep. You know, cut it off."

"Fur isn't like wool. It's no good unless it's stuck to something — like skin — so it's all in one piece." Vicky dug in her jeans and thrust a folded piece of paper at him. It was a copy of a magazine picture.

Skip screwed up his face. "So?"

"Read what it says underneath," Vicky persisted. "Lynn's grandmother says Rudy and Cleo are bobcats, right?"

Skip had been enthusiastic when Vicky first gave him the news, but now he approached the information like an animal sniffing the bait. "Yeah."

"Those are dead bobcats."

"E-e-e-ow!" Skip held the picture close to examine the fence. "Howie wouldn't do that," he said with conviction.

"He catches them and sells them so somebody else can do that." Vicky poked the piece of paper. "They're just as dead either way."

Skip was steadfast. "Howie wouldn't do that."

"Is he down at the beach?" Vicky set out, bent on confrontation. "We'll ask him."

Lynn suddenly was feeling ridiculous. She did not have one shred of evidence: only overheard conversation and a lot of guesses. She tried to restrain Vicky. "If we make him mad and he finds Cleo, he'll be sure not to give her back," she warned.

Vicky halted briefly. "The thing that burns me is he pretended to be so interested. I want him to know we know, that's all," and Vicky plunged down the hill.

She descended on Howie like a raging tornado, and the argument was every bit as nasty as Lynn feared it would be, though Howie never once denied the accusations.

Most girls would not have done it, particularly not against an older guy. But Vicky managed to snare Howie in such a way that he could not simply abandon the battle; he had to prove he was right.

"What's one less cat to you?" Howie needled Vicky. "You don't live around here. At the end of the summer you'll dump them. Summer people do it all the time."

"Fat chance we'll dump them. Don't you wish. You just stay off our property."

"You think that's going to matter when you're gone to New York? What if you don't find her before then?" Howie raised both hands as if he were about to be arrested. "Honest, officer, the trap was on this side of the line and the cat walked right in."

"It may be legal. That doesn't make it right," shouted Vicky.

"What's that supposed to mean?"

"It's dirty money."

Howie laughed too loud for it to be funny. "What's clean money?"

"You can get a job. Earn it some other way."

"I suppose when your mother and father give it to you it's clean. I don't get handouts. Neither do Chris and Joe. So we have to get it the best way we can." Howie was one-up for the moment. He pressed his advantage. "I could say you stole those kittens from me."

"Baloney. We found them on our property."

"If I had the mother first, those kittens belong to me."

Vicky eyed him coolly. "You had her first, all right. Had her — past tense. You didn't know and you didn't care if she had kittens."

"What's this 'past tense' garbage? Maybe I still have her."

"Oh yeah? Then show me!" Vicky exploded. "If she's still around, it's limp on somebody's back." Howie was silent. "You didn't care about her or her kittens," Vicky repeated. "If we find any more traps, we'll dump them in the pond. Now stay off our property." It was Vicky's final warning.

"Make me."

Up to now Skip had been standing to one side, chewing his fingernails. He joined his sister. He looked up at Howie. "You stink," he said.

Howie's face turned scarlet. "What do you know, shortstop?" he mumbled. Howie slipped on his helmet and drove off.

With the aid of a flashlight Vicky dug around in the odds and ends stored under the guest house. She pulled out a rusted shovel and several orange life preservers, then she found what she was looking for, a sign an older cousin had made when she first learned to read. The nail heads were bent and twisted sideways into the wood. STAY OFF, it said. PRIVATE BEACH. Her cousin had explained what the sign meant and Vicky remembered staring up at the words, so powerful they could turn people away.

It was nearly dark when she pounded the sign into the sand on the exact line between their property and the public beach and dragged stones from the garden to pile around it. It wouldn't accomplish a thing, but it made her feel better.

17

❧❧❧

"I bet she's starving," said Skip, as he sat with Lynn on the porch swing. It was three days now since Cleo was seen last.

"She'll learn to hunt her food quick enough," said Grammer. "Even if she loses a few squirrels, she can make out okay. It's summer and there's plenty of food in the woods."

"How do you know so much about bobcats, Mrs. Davis?" asked Skip.

Grammer closed one eye and looked over her glasses at Skip with the other, deciding whether or not she should answer. "It comes with the territory — the same way you know about those underground trains, which is something I'll never get the hang of. Or care to." She folded her arms and closed down the other eyelid. Grammer was more herself today — tired perhaps, but herself.

"If that Howie boy finds her first," Grammer continued, "he'll have to board her until she winters out. She's no use to him as young as she is. I imagine he knows that."

Howie had not appeared today either. Chris and Joe had been at the beach earlier, asking about him. He was not at his house, they said. The boys hung around the parking lot, riding their dirt bikes into the water. Finally, they had pedaled off. Maybe Howie was avoiding them as well.

"Hi." Vicky came up to the porch. She was carrying Rudy, who growled and tried to squirm up onto her shoulder. He turned his head and bit. "Ow!" Vicky got a firm hold on the leash and let him drop to the ground. His headlong escape was cut short after a few feet and he flopped on his side.

"Let me have him," said Skip.

"No, he's been carried around too much." Whenever they went into the woods looking for Cleo, they brought Rudy along, hoping he would detect her scent somehow and lead them to her. At first there was a certain amount of tail switching, but after three days of constant handling he was plainly disagreeable.

Everyone had been out to hunt for Cleo at one time or another: Nan and Doug combed areas Vicky and Skip had already covered, searching for something they might have missed; Justin and Glory wandered west of the cove; Lynn rode as far as the next couple of crossroads, stopping every few yards to investigate the side of the road. Even Grammer scoured her memory for possible hiding places, some of which they found did not exist anymore.

131

Vicky watched as Rudy tangled his paws in the leash. They had run out of ideas; she was running low on steam, and maybe hope; and there was not one sign of Cleo.

"Nan says you're both invited to dinner. Want to come?" Vicky asked almost as an afterthought.

"Sure," said Lynn. "Grammer?"

"I think I'll set here on the porch till it cools a bit." She nodded to Skip. "Maybe you'll come up later, and you bring that game with you, eh?" Grammer was referring to Comet Chasers, Skip's electronic game. From the first she had marveled at it.

It was not anything Lynn would have predicted would interest Grammer — she was not overly impressed by the twentieth century, as she put it once — but if you could predict one thing about Grammer, it was that she was unpredictable. "Grammer, you're turning into a beep freak," Lynn teased.

"Get on with you," Grammer objected good-naturedly. "The whole peck and passel of you."

"Anything wrong?" Nan asked.

"No, she's probably gone to bed. She gets up very early in the morning," said Lynn. She was phoning Grammer to invite her for a few rounds of Charades. Justin and Glory were there, eager to play. The Seymours' games always were free-wheeling and hotly contested, particularly Charades, since they allowed anything — single words, camp songs, recipes.

Lynn dialed again. Out in the other room they were debating placing a notice for Cleo in the Lost and Found column of the paper.

"Terrific," said Vicky, "and we advertise a stray bobcat

for every other person like Howie who can't wait to get his hands on her fur. Forget it."

Again no answer. Lynn hung up. She hesitated, then said to Nan, "I just want to go up and see."

"Of course. We can clear the dishes until you come back. Tell her we need her," Nan said as Lynn was leaving.

"I will."

Lynn was feeling anxious as she mounted Smoke, though she didn't know why. She tried to put it out of her mind by focusing on the shapes and sounds outside her. The lighting abruptly changed once she left the Seymours' path and guided Smoke into the dense black trees. Edges disappeared and the trail blurred into night. Only the slimmest moonlit strands seemed to thread the branches to touch the ground.

Finally, her eyes adapted to the dark and she was feeling a little less uneasy. She bent low over Smoke's mane and jabbed her heels. He picked up the pace briefly, then slowed as they turned uphill. At the crest of the hill he halted. His ears flickered. Lynn thought she heard a rustling but she could not see anything. Probably a small animal running across the trail. "C'mon, boy."

They were crossing the meadow. Light was coming from the living room and kitchen of the farmhouse. Lynn was trying to puzzle out what that meant. Grammer would have left only the porchlight on if she were in bed.

She had decided not to bother stopping to tie up Smoke at the barn, when it happened.

There was a sharp crack. Lynn knew instantly it was a gun. How many times had she watched Grammer line up the cans? It was nothing like a car backfiring, the way people imagined. A horse whinnied. It sounded far off, but it was her horse. She was pitched sideways. The rocky soil rose up and met her arm and shoulder with a dull thud. It was over both so fast and so slowly — her body spun out of control, her mind piecing together fragments.

"Lord above, help me," she heard her grandmother cry. "It's Smoke."

Then darkness collapsed in on her with a roar.

18

✿✿✿

After nearly three days in the hospital with the nurses coming and going at all hours, Lynn had lost track of time. It was as if the night of the accident never ended. And now her mother was here. At least Lynn was back home at Grammer's.

Lynn pulled herself to a sitting position on the couch. With her arm in a cast it was awkward. The pain-killers were wearing off. She was tempted to ask for more, but she hated that fogged-in feeling.

"Is this yours?" her mother asked, holding a navy turtleneck at arm's length. She was doing laundry, while Lynn rested until she felt well enough to travel.

Lynn raged inside. Of course it's mine. You know Grammer wears housedresses, she wanted to sneer.

"I don't like you in dark colors. Why didn't you buy

one of those print turtlenecks? The ones all the girls are wearing with the sweet little flowers or frogs, hm?"

Her mother clacked briskly to the kitchen. That was so typical. Bustle. Bustle. Bustle. Her mother was always busy getting things done: Junior Women's, the Antique Show, Friends of the Library, raising money for one thing or another. Too busy to hear how Lynn really broke her elbow.

She would have felt like a clown in one of those cutesy numbers with the red hearts. "Mom," Lynn called irritably. "Mom!"

"You don't have to shout," she said, heels clacking.

"I need another pain pill."

Her mother sighed. "I guess I won't be able to get you home as soon as I'd planned."

"It hurts."

"I'm sure it does." Her mother patted her the way people pat a puppy. "If your grandmother had put away that gun when your father told her — She could have shot you!" Her mother shuddered. "At least she had the sense to call the Seymours. Honestly, I don't know how you've endured it all summer. She's so cranky and unreasonable. Your father should sell the farm and put her in a home."

"Forget it."

"Forget what?" her mother said, stiffening.

Lynn considered having it out with her. Grammer was not to blame. And she was not senile. But between the ache and the fatigue — and force of habit — she did not feel strong enough. "For a minute I thought I didn't want my pill. On second thought, I do." Her mother patted her again. Down dog. Good dog.

She returned quickly with Lynn's medicine. "By the way, those hippie friends of your grandmother's stopped by."

"They're my friends, too."

"I see," her mother answered coolly.

Lynn swallowed her pill and put down the glass. "I know what you're thinking and they're not like that. They're teachers. On summer vacation."

"Teachers?" Her mother was incredulous. "In some hillbilly school."

"If it weren't for the way Glory and Justin took care of my arm, Dr. Noyes said I would have needed surgery."

"Am I being ungrateful? I suppose so. Forgive me. In any case, Glory — is that her real name? — Glory said she'd stop again later."

Lynn felt warm, beginning to slip into the fog. Why was everything so awful suddenly? It was her fault Grammer was in trouble. If only she had whistled, given some warning. Grammer didn't expect her, coming on the back trail. And now she had to go home. She wished her pill could take care of other kinds of pain besides a broken elbow.

Vicky listed every reason she could think of for why she should be happy. Maybe that would help shake the gloom. One. Lynn was hurt, but okay. She had to stay in the hospital until the swelling went down and they could put on a real cast, but she was okay. Two. Smoke was okay. He was only frightened and reared when the bullet whizzed past. Three. And Cleo was okay.

It was the creepiest sensation in the world to have Cleo come back like that. After the commotion of Lynn's going to the hospital, Vicky was putting Smoke in the barn for the night — and there she was, in the straw, waking up from a nap. They might as well have enjoyed themselves the whole time, instead of worrying. Everyone seemed to assume Cleo had been in the barn all along but Vicky wasn't buying it. Not three days.

Three good reasons and still Vicky felt gloomy.

The toilet flushed. Skip's slippers flop-flopped down the hall. "Look at this," he said, holding out the pages she had copied at the library. "It says here wildcats are simple to trap. They walk right in."

Vicky knew without looking which picture it was. The one of a bewildered pair of eyes from inside a cage. The animal didn't know what hit him.

"Not Cleo," said Skip. "She was too smart to get caught."

"I wouldn't bet on it."

"Huh?" Skip was absorbed in a peanut butter and pickle sandwich.

"For breakfast? Yucch."

"Mm-mm." Skip smacked his lips.

Vicky's chin sagged onto her fists as she stared at the picture Skip had dropped. Cleo was as much a prisoner as those eyes. She had come back, but what good did it do? To keep the cats safe they were tying them to a post in the yard by day and cooping them up in the barn by night. The cats were not only safe, they were miserable.

She remembered Skip's poor snake, the one that baked in the car. "Maybe this tells us something," Nan had said. At the time Vicky decided it was that death was disgusting, but she understood now why Nan wanted to wait for the mother cat to return to her kittens in the canoe.

If they had left the snake where it was, everyone would have continued to coexist: the people in their niche, the snake in his, something living, unowned and separate.

Vicky knew Rudy and Cleo were different, and she ignored it; she wanted them to come to New York so badly. Both she and Skip did. She had really believed she could change them, that it was okay to change them. She was wrong. But knowing it didn't help much.

"Hey, Skip?" she said quietly. "I've been thinking. We can't keep Rudy and Cleo. It would be an awful mistake." Vicky let the idea penetrate, then she tried to offer a reason he would understand. "For one thing they don't make good pets."

"Rudy's a great pet. So is Cleo."

"Don't argue. Just listen, will you? I found a lot about them in the library. They aren't too bad now — well, bad enough for Mom to throw them out of the house. In a couple of years they can get super-mean."

"Who says?"

"Everyone, practically. There was an article a vet wrote. Someone gave him a bobcat to be destroyed, but he kept it. They ended up, they had to put it to sleep. Some little girl let it out of its pen. She was carrying a parakeet. The cat went berserk and clawed the little girl by mistake. There was exactly one story that told about a bobcat making a good pet, and they said it was unusual."

"Maybe — "

"Aww, Skip, face it. How many kids in our building have canaries or gerbils or guinea pigs? They're on the elevator all the time."

"They're in cages."

"Do you want Randy or Karen to get hurt because one

of our cats goes nuts jumping at the cage? That's what happened to the girl with the bird."

"No."

"Neither do I. That's the trouble. I hate being responsible," said Vicky. "It's a pain right in the be-hind. You're lucky you're not older."

"But we were going to civilize them — so they wouldn't do that."

"We can't civilize them. They don't belong with us. They belong someplace where they can be bobcats."

She pulled Skip down into a chair. "You remember what Harp the Carp was like?"

"Yeah," said Skip, puzzled. "Mean."

"No, more than that. What did she make you feel like?"

"Crummy."

"What did Danny do? You were always complaining about Danny."

"Danny used to butter her up."

"And if you buttered her up, what did you feel like?"

"Not me! I didn't do it."

Vicky eyeballed him. "Not ever?"

Skip reconsidered. "All right. Once."

"How did you feel?" Vicky pressed.

"Like a jerk. What else?"

"Relax." Vicky patted Skip. "We all did it to get her off our backs." This was not working. She tried a different tack. "Okay. Suppose somebody is trying to turn you into someone else, like a robot, telling you what to think or what to do all the time, and you don't have a vote on it. Like in history. Can you remember anything like that?"

"Yeah. Lots of things."

"Good. Like what?"

"When you make me learn the Presidents and study vocabulary and all that stuff."

Vicky was stung. "What do you mean, Skip?"

"Well, you try to make me be like you, and I don't have a vote on it. And it's like you think I'm a robot or something. And it makes me mad, and I wish you'd leave me alone, so I can do what I want to do, and not feel like I'm a criminal all the time."

This was not exactly what Vicky had in mind. She swallowed hard and said, "I think we're making the cats feel like that. Like they're being punished."

"I get it," said Skip. "And they don't even know what they did that was so wrong. Like Mrs. Harper. She sure made you think you'd done something wrong, just for breathing."

Skip's face clouded all of a sudden. "But if we can't keep Rudy and Cleo, what are we going to do with them?"

"We'll think of something," Vicky said resolutely.

Skip was right. The way she treated him was the same. She had really believed she could change him, that it was okay to change him. She took a deep breath. Vicky in her niche. Skip in his. Separate and unowned. Not her. Not a robot.

After they were dressed and had dropped off a letter at the mailbox for Nan, Skip suggested they continue up the road to see Lynn. Lynn was sleeping, so they visited a few minutes on the porch with Mrs. Davis. She may have needed a visitor more than Lynn, Vicky thought. She seemed so alone, even with Billy curled beside her chair.

Skip explained their new plans for the cats and that they

wanted a place for them where they were safe but could run, too. Did she have any ideas?

"Free and safe," murmured Mrs. Davis. "Not easy to come by both." Her look darkened. "They're God's own creatures, but they're bad luck. Bobs never brought me a stitch of good. Lookit what they did. Barely missed killing my own granddaughter."

She closed her eyes, humming pieces of tunes, repeating them several times, then she raised herself heavily out of her rocker and went inside without an excuse or a good-bye. She had forgotten they were there.

"Is that what you want to do?" Glory asked Lynn.

Did Glory really not know? Of course she didn't want to leave. She didn't have a choice. Her mother had it orga-nized already: her luggage, how they would get to Logan Airport in Boston, a visiting nurse to look in on Grammer. And on. And on.

Grammer came out of her bedroom. Her movements were careful, her rounded shoulders stooped still lower. She had barely spoken a word to Lynn since the acci-dent — and now she hardly seemed to notice her. They watched her plod on to the kitchen. The door squeaked and swung closed.

The voices were muffled, but Lynn guessed Grammer was telling her mother she was ready to go into a nursing home. She could hear her mother. "You'll love it . . . for the best, Mother Davis." The look on Glory's face con-firmed it. Lynn wanted to gag.

"I have something for you," Glory said and held out the ball of yarn from her trunk. "Neat, isn't it, the way it catches the light and gives it back." She placed the yarn in Lynn's good hand. "It's yours. Use it, kiddo."

Lynn frowned. What could she mean by that?

"The dog was a dumb, obedient mutt," said Glory, "but he was also this. Something beautiful and unusual. This is wildcatting — seeing through what everyone knows to be there, to what else is possible."

Lynn sank against the pillows. She was too tired to be bothered with riddles.

The springs of Skip's cot twanged in the dark. Vicky was having a hard time falling asleep, too. Things were so much up in the air with the cats. But that was not all that was keeping her awake. She wished she could make some sort of apology to Skip, but she had broken so many promises already, there was not much point in making another.

"Anything the matter?" Vicky asked after a few more twangs.

Skip propped himself on an elbow. "I know we can't keep them, but I wish we could."

"Me too."

He lay back on his pillow. "You know all that stuff I said about you thinking I was a robot? That isn't all the time. Only when it's too hard or I don't want to know it."

"Oh." That made her feel a little less like a monster. "Thanks, Skip, for telling me."

Skip climbed out of bed and turned on the light. Vicky covered her eyes. "Skip!"

He dropped onto the end of her bed. "You know the subtraction game where you can always tell me the answer?"

"Yes." It was a strange thing to bring up now.

"Would you teach it to me?"

Vicky sat up. "Sure. It's a trick, in that book from the Smithsonian. See, the number nine has special properties — Wait, let's get some paper and I'll show you." Vicky started out of bed, then stopped. "You positive?" Skip nodded. "Tell me if it gets boring."

He extended a hand and they slapped five, first one hand, then the other. Vicky thought of her list of good things. Add Number Four. Vicky and Skip were going to be okay.

19

❦❦❦

They were not leaving right away for New Jersey, Lynn's mother cheerfully explained in the morning. They were staying through to Labor Day so that she could organize things for Grammer to go into a nursing home.

Lynn wanted to rage — at her mother for treating this like another one of her antique shows, and at Grammer for giving in. She pushed unannounced into the dingy gray of Grammer's room. Grammer was sitting beside the half-drawn shade, idly flipping the corners of a book. In her lap lay the only patch of sunlight to reach beyond the window. Then Lynn saw the tears tracing thin lines on her cheeks.

"We've had quite a summer, haven't we, child," her grandmother whispered. "Here, sit alongside."

Grammer had lost so much weight, Lynn realized

abruptly, that she could squeeze into the overstuffed chair with her. "Feels like old times," said Grammer. "We used to sit here until you got too big for lap-sitting. So we went to porch-sitting like the grown folks. Porch-sitting is fine, but once in a while a person needs a good lap-sitting.

"Used to be, people took sick, some with stroke, or pneumonia, or some sick of living, and they'd prop them in a straight chair by the woodstove or in a bed off the kitchen. Family did most of what doctoring there was. While you were grumbling over your aches, you shelled peas for your daughter's supper and you teased the little ones, and you died right there in plain view of everybody."

"You're not going to die."

"Not today. I'm too stubborn," said Grammer. "But I've been stubborn past the time when I should."

"You're not even sick."

Grammer pulled Lynn closer, being careful not to squeeze the injured arm. "Lovie, I've had my warning."

"What warning?"

"You remember the woman over in Center Sandwich drove through a stop sign, killed a little girl?"

Lynn remembered. She remembered most how it upset Grammer.

"I swore myself an oath — I'd give up driving at the first sign if the Lord would spare me that pitiful lady's torment. I never dreamed it to come with my gun. He spared us both, child. I find it hard enough to live with myself knowing I hurt you, without risking more harm."

"It was an accident. You told me yourself — you saw a light by the barn." Lynn had thought about what happened that night dozens of times. Grammer saw the light and went out with her gun. She was aiming for the rooster, the weathervane, to frighten whoever it was away. Then Lynn had come up behind her. It was a stupid accident!

"No telling what I saw," Grammer lamented. "I knew I'd mistook, when I turned about, but I couldn't alter what was in motion. Like her — putting her foot on the gas. There's no kicking the thing under the bed. The next time it could be me with the car."

Lynn leapt from the chair. "That's no reason to go to a home."

"I can't stay on here without a car. It's but a matter of time, child."

There was an excited rapping at the door. "I called The Alcove, Mother Davis. They can take you! They're converting a house next door to a dormitory. You might have to double up for a few weeks. I'm sure you don't mind. It's an excellent way to get acquainted." Lynn's mother beamed. "Oh, I knew putting our name on the waiting list was the right thing."

"You're both nuts," said Lynn. "I've seen those places. They're awful."

"Lynn, don't be fresh. Your grandmother was very ill this last spring. She needs care — "

"Yeah — not a coffin!"

Lynn's mother reeled at the outburst. Usually when they fought it was polite battle, with pinpricks and needles. "I'm not listening to this," she said when she recovered her composure.

Lynn stomped outside.

The Good Shepherd, that was the name. She visited it in Girl Scouts, before she quit. Each Christmas two or three of the mothers drove them across the river into Paterson, past high-walled schoolyards and factories to a shabby white house with a slanted porch and a ramp. A tinsel garland was draped over the sign, THE GOOD SHEPHERD. The girls were ushered into a narrow corridor, where they sang Christmas carols, while the patients stood in the doorways and watched in their slippers and nightgowns. Five o'clock in the afternoon and they were dressed for bed.

"What we need is a preservation," said Skip, bouncing on his bed.

"What's that?" Vicky laughed.

"A reservation to preserve wildcats. And not a zoo," said Skip.

Vicky snapped to attention. "Wait a minute! There are wildlife sanctuaries, where they keep animals safe from hunters and cars — and — " She riffled through the papers, then raced to the box where she had stored the others. "Phooey. I didn't copy it."

Vicky yelled down to Nan at her typewriter. "Can I have a ride to the library?" She paused long enough for an answer. "Five minutes." Vicky twirled her brother in a dance. "Skip, you did it! There's a man, and he studies wildcats. But it's on a preserve. That means nobody can trap them, except the scientists! And they only do it to measure them."

"What?"

"I read a story he wrote. He's going to want Rudy and Cleo. I know it!"

"I'm coming with you," said Skip, charging ahead to the attic stairs.

When they returned from town Vicky and Skip pored over every word of the magazine article. This Dr. Bennett

146

sounded like the right person. He was studying social behavior in wildcats. He thought maybe the cats lived in families. He wasn't interested in cutting up their brains or any of that business.

A man from their father's college had taken their family on a tour of the Brain Lab once. He said when they were finished experimenting with the animals they put them to sleep and dissected their brain tissue. Mostly it was huge computers on the tour. Vicky was glad they did not see where they sacrificed them, as he had called it.

To make certain about Dr. Bennett they asked in their letter to him if he sacrificed any of the animals after his research was done.

Other than that part, Vicky thought it was a very positive letter. In language arts class, her teacher emphasized that positive arguments were stronger than negative ones, so Vicky described all the good points. They were young, healthy animals and since the preserve was practically next door in Maine, the cats already were used to the weather. Also, he would be able to study if bobcats adopted other cats, the way people do. This last was Skip's idea. Vicky thought it was pretty poor, but after the pact she had made with herself, she was not about to criticize. Besides, it couldn't hurt if Dr. Bennett saw they were trying to help with his research.

They hurried to the mailbox and turned up the red flag. A loud hooray from Skip pierced the air. There was the rural mail truck, spinning a cloud of dust from its rear wheels.

That weekend Lynn's mother drove Grammer's Dodge into Meredith, where she rented a newer car. Grammer fussed, but only about leaving the Dodge, and early Monday they were headed south for Hartford, Connecticut, and the home.

Swatches of blue lake drifted beside Lynn's window. She had tried to beg off this trip, but her mother would not hear of it. "For your own peace of mind, dear, I want you to see where your grandmother will be living." Her mother patted Grammer's knee. "We'll see lots more of you, Mother Davis. Our friend Mrs. Warren has a mother staying there. It's a lovely place. Really, it's a misnomer to call it a nursing home. It's a residence."

Hours of superlatives and small talk until her mother drove through an open gate and announced this was it.

Lynn waited with Grammer in the lounge, while her mother spoke to the receptionist. A white-haired, bearded man with a big red nose was tending the plants. He could have been Santa Claus. With enormous care, he fluffed and arranged the leaves and snipped away the dead ones.

They saw cheery rooms, well-manicured grounds, a patio with wide-brimmed umbrellas where several people, some of them in wheelchairs, were sitting with nurses. The woman who showed them about was polite, efficient, not cloying, as the aides at The Good Shepherd had been. She pointed out the colonial-style house next door. "Our patients in the annexes are able to get up and down stairs, of course. You'll notice here," she said, referring to the brick building behind them, "everything's on ground level and accessible by ramp. The more severely limited patients live here."

Almost on cue, a tall woman, her hair braided around her head like a dark halo, broke from the group on the patio. She half-pushed, half-carried an aluminum frame that supported her as she walked up the short ramp and inside.

The aide invited them to stay for lunch. Meals were served family style, five or six people at a table. Lynn was beginning to wish she could find just one thing to hate about the place. She should have known her mother would never embarrass herself by putting Grammer in a dump like The Good Shepherd.

They found Mrs. Warren's mother in one of the annexes. She was watching TV with several other people. Her mother introduced them. She was very sweet, eager to please.

Lynn's mother obviously was trying to kindle some sort of interest between Grammer and this woman. She was asking her what kinds of activities were planned for residents and what she liked to do best. "Oh, mostly I watch the soap operas." Mrs. Warren's mother laughed shyly. "We all do."

Grammer's face soured. She had so little patience for television she gave away the only set she owned to the church bazaar.

Lynn wandered out into the hall in time to see the Santa Claus man. "Hi," she said. "Your plants are very nice."

The man brought his face so close to Lynn's she backed away. "They say I'm dangerous. Kept here against my will, and *I'm* the one who's dangerous," he clucked, then continued into the lounge where he stood in front of the television watchers until an aide led him aside.

Fortunately, her mother was ready.

"Any questions before you leave?" a nurse addressed Grammer.

Grammer surveyed her audience. "Yes, I have one,"

she said, tasting her words. "Tell me, in a good year, how many of your guests do you bury?" Then she snickered. Lynn's mother seethed.

They arrived back at Grammer's farm late in the afternoon. Because of her sling, Lynn couldn't ride, but she could escape to the cove. She watched her mother out of the corner of her eye, half waiting for her to object, as she found bread for the birds. Her mother was making a point, however, of ignoring them both, which meant no questions at least.

Outside, Billy danced at Lynn's feet, delighted with the prospect of a walk.

The cove seemed drab without Justin and Glory's big blue blossom of a tent. Leaving Billy and some of their excess gear behind, they had made a quick trip to China, Maine, where Justin's finger originally touched the map. They were planning to come back in a week or so, stay a few days, then pack up for Illinois in time to get ready for the opening of school.

Glory must have sensed she would need a friend. Lynn sat in the sand and let Billy romp and lick her face. Then she unhooked his collar and he dashed straight into a covey of birds that took to the sky, squawking angrily.

The day's events chased round and round, replaying things the guide nurse had said. Everything had been "patients" this, "patients" that. Lynn tossed the bread carelessly on the sand. Grammer was not a patient.

She called to Billy. The dog loped to her side and allowed himself to be leashed. Coming round the point from the cove, she could see a few people on the beach picnicking. There was no evidence of Howie — no dirt bikes or moped.

The longer he stayed away the more certain she was: It was Howie with the light Grammer saw by the barn. She knew it down to the pit of her stomach. Cleo's return was too coincidental otherwise.

If only he had picked some other way to bring her back, but Lynn also knew perfectly well why he did it — because he couldn't stand up and admit to them he had her. He probably would not be back to the beach again until they went home.

Lynn started up the Seymours' path. It was where she had intended to go all along. Without her mother here, she would not have left Grammer by herself. And deep down, Lynn knew that was what Grammer was trying to tell her — that she was afraid to be alone.

Darn that Howie!

20

❧❧❧

Maybe it was because they had written to this Dr. Bennett that Vicky expected his reply to be by letter. When the phone rang, she was sure it was Doug calling from New York to let them know when he'd be arriving for the weekend. He'd had to return early for some sort of a committee meeting at school, then he was coming back up to stay until Labor Day. Vicky was going to ask him to bring fresh bagels when she realized that the man at the other end did not sound anything like her father.

"Hello? Um. Is this the Seymour residence? I'm trying

to reach either Victoria or Charles Seymour. My name is Roger Bennett."

Vicky gulped. He must have phoned as soon as he read the letter. "Yes," she said, in her most grown-up voice, "this is Victoria Seymour."

Dr. Bennett relaxed immediately. "Good. I tried only one other Seymour." He laughed. The laugh was thin and high-pitched, stretched over the miles. "These cats you have — you're certain, are you, these are genuine? People sometimes think what they have are bobcats and they're feral cats, that is, runaways or lost housecats."

"Yes sir, I'm certain. I looked them up at the library."

"Yes, of course. You mentioned that." He paused. "All right, if it's convenient for you and your family, I'd like to drive your way this next weekend and take a look for myself. I can't pay you, but if your animals are bobcats, I'd like to bring them back with me." There was another blank space, then he said, "I can't make guarantees. The animals are protected: We inoculate them, we do all we can, but they do catch diseases and injure themselves. They're in their natural habitat, not the safety of a home."

"Yes sir. That's what we want."

"Fine." Dr. Bennett gave Vicky his phone number and asked her to check with her family and it was over.

He wanted them.

"Mom says lunch is ready, and why don't you come eat with us in the kitchen."

"I'm not hungry," Grammer answered, dismissing her. Lynn took her usual place, cross-legged at the end of the bed. Grammer looked up. "You're staying put, I see." She laid down her book and removed her reading glasses.

They dangled from a chain around her neck. "How's your arm doing?"

"It doesn't hurt anymore."

"Well, that cheers me a great deal. What else is new? Justin have a good hike on Chocorua?" Justin and Glory were back, and Justin was so car-weary he vowed he would never make it to the Midwest unless he climbed a mountain first.

"He says his shins hurt like crazy. I saw them out in the water. Glory's pretending she's a whirlpool."

"I could have told him he hadn't toughened his legs enough. You don't do Rattlesnake one day and Chocorua the next." Grammer laughed. "My, but I'll miss that pair and their goings on."

"I wonder if they'll come back next summer," said Lynn.

Grammer's hand flicked irritably. "I won't be here to see it." Grammer lifted her chin. She looked at Lynn from the eyes on the tip of her nose. "Is that what you come here to talk about?"

"You could change your mind, Grammer," Lynn blurted. "If you said so, Daddy wouldn't let her make you do something you don't want to."

"Child, what I want can't be done."

Lynn's head drooped. She fiddled with a tassel on the afghan.

Grammer sat beside her, quieting Lynn's hand with hers. "I'll make out there. 'Course I'll have to learn how to be snooty and when you visit I'll introduce you as Lynn Davis the Third," she joked.

"It's not that country club your mother's picked out," Grammer said, getting up to look out the window. "It's all this I'm grieving over. There'll be people after your father to sell the farm, as soon as I move out, and when it becomes nothing except a bother to him, he'll have to give in. Pretty soon it's cut up into bitty parts and they're taking down these hills, where a person hiked and hunted for jack-in-the-pulpits and maybe fell in love with a man, until a body doesn't recognize it. On the far side of the pond, your grandfather's proposing spot is a glass house. I don't know how they heat the darned thing.

"Well." Grammer grabbed Lynn's toes. Lynn played the game and struggled. "How about bringing in some of that gour-met stuff your mother calls lunch? Then you scoot. Smoke could use a workout. Go over and see if Vicky will oblige." She grimaced. "I could show your mother a thing or two in the kitchen about stick-to-your-ribs cooking. Careful of that arm."

"Is she still locking herself in her room?" Glory asked Lynn.

"She comes out for meals, but not always. Mom says Grammer's just acting spoiled — to make her feel guilty." Lynn made it clear she thought her mother was the one acting spoiled.

"She probably does feel guilty," said Glory. "I would."

Nan, Glory, Vicky, and Lynn were sitting around the Seymours' picnic table, sipping iced tea. Despite the differences in age and dress, they wove together into a strangely soothing circle of talk. Lynn supposed it was a ladies' coffee klatch, but she liked it anyway.

"Who knows what might have happened to her if you hadn't been here, Lynn," said Nan. "I wouldn't want her wandering, lost and dizzy, and no one's realizing she was missing until it's too late."

Lynn drank her tea, hiding for a moment. Nan had pretty much figured out what occurred that awful night Grammer lost the kittens.

"What does your dad say?" Vicky asked.

Lynn came out from behind the glass. "He says my mother and grandmother could never live together. He wanted my mother to find a live-in housekeeper. But she says she isn't running up every couple of weeks to hire someone new." Lynn explained the trouble they'd had keeping housekeepers while Grammer was recovering from pneumonia.

Justin came limping from the beach. "Ohh," he complained, "whoever said climbing back down to the bottom was the simple part must have been another Illini. What do foreigners from the Midwest know about mountains? The second day, and I hurt worse." He collapsed into the lounge chair. "It sure was pretty, though, on top of that mountain. Like you could reach out and hold a fistful of heaven. Wish I could take some of that home with me."

"Stay here," said Nan, "and you can reach for your fistful whenever you feel like it. That and your stupendous broccoli," she ribbed him. Justin had nurtured a particularly large head, which he wouldn't harvest, until Grammer made him cut it before it went to seed.

"Mrs. Davis is looking for a housekeeper," Vicky suggested.

"I'll take it. Private Dustmop reporting for duty —sir!" Justin saluted and tried to spring to his feet, but his stiff muscles would not cooperate. He fell backward into the chair. "Ahh — wounded in action," he cried.

"Clown." Glory dove into Justin, tickling until he begged for mercy. "This is serious," she scolded. Justin outlined a box in the air and pointed at Glory. Glory mugged. "Same to you, fella."

"I thought your grandmother's going to Connecticut was settled," asked Justin.

"It is. Unless Grammer changes her mind."

"Any chance of that?"

"No."

"That's tough," he said. "I can't see your grandmother in a home. She'll be like one of those birds caught in an oil spill."

"And yet she shouldn't live alone," Nan reminded them.

"It's tough," Justin repeated.

Nan must have noticed that Lynn was starting to feel glum; she maneuvered the conversation around to an end-of-summer cookout. "We'll do it up right. A real shindig," said Nan.

"Great! A blowout," Justin said to Glory.

Vicky elbowed Lynn. "They mean a party." Lynn smiled. Having people on your side helped.

"C'mon down."

Vicky dismounted, happy to be on solid ground again. She felt as if she had ridden Smoke for hours.

"What's wrong?" asked Lynn. "You weren't as relaxed this time. A horse won't know you're boss if you're scared."

"Are you kidding?" said Vicky. "I'm spooked seeing you in that cast."

The two girls walked the horse inside the paddock. After a week of too little exercise, Smoke was frisky. Vicky held the reins. "Whoa," she called, giggling. "On the ground, I'm in charge."

"Do you think you'll want to keep riding in the fall?" Lynn asked. 'With my grandmother giving up the farm I'll have to board Smoke around home. You could take a bus out to New Jersey and we'd ride together."

Vicky hesitated. She liked Lynn a lot. She was her first high school friend who wasn't a babysitter. Vicky didn't want to do anything to wreck it, but if they had to go horseback riding every time, it would end up wrecked anyway.

"Everything sounded terrific," Vicky began, "until you got to the part about riding." Vicky patted Smoke's muzzle. "Sorry, pal. Heights make me nervous." She looked to Lynn. "I appreciate your trying, really I do, but I'm beyond hope — I hate the World Trade Center, too, and airplanes." She thought of Skip. "It's no fun doing it, when you know you'll always be scared and crummy. What if you take the bus into the city once in a while?"

"Chinatown?" said Lynn. "I love the dumpling houses and the Oriental grocery stores."

"I know a fabulous record store near there," said Vicky. "It's about a ten-minute walk."

"It's a deal."

Justin waved on his way to do some last minute repairs for Grammer. The girls waved back. "You know," Vicky said as he disappeared inside the barn, "my Aunt Rae has someone to live in with her, sort of like a housekeeper, only not really. She's a college student. She does some of the cleaning and the cooking and she gets her room free. Aunt Rae says she's a pretty terrible cook, but she doesn't care because she likes her. The hang-up before was that your grandmother didn't like anyone your mother got, right?"

"Grammer said they were too nosy."

"Glory and Justin would be perfect. She really likes them, and they really like her. It's simple."

Lynn wished it were. "You don't know my mother. She has a headache every time Justin or Glory comes up to the house. She'd never go for it."

"Ask her at least."

"Forget it," said Lynn. "I met one of them my mother hired, and she was Barracuda Lady. My mother loved her, and when Grammer fired her, it was the last straw."

It was almost unfair the way the cats were so easy to walk today, now that they weren't going to keep them. Cleo and Rudy loped ahead of Vicky and Skip, their leashes dangling. Occasionally, one of the cats halted to mark a tree or bush with urine, then smoothly resumed the pace. They took the path off Deerhill Road to the blueberry bushes, and farther on, to a ridge jutting into the water. From here Deerhill Pond appeared limitless, curling around the stand of giant pines to the cove and skyward.

The cats gnawed on stalks of grasses that poked out of the rocky crevices. When they tired of the weeds, they wrestled. They slapped, climbed, and vaulted, one over the other. A paw would snap and suddenly the second cat would charge, then stop short, teetering on the edge of an actual battle.

Skip untangled their lines and he and Vicky pulled the cats apart, coaxing them to sit in the sun. Skip stroked and stroked Cleo's coarse fur until she caught his hand in her jaw lightly, as if to say enough.

"Why can't he wait until Labor Day?" Skip was talking about Dr. Bennett, who was coming the last weekend in August.

"Maybe he wanted to avoid the traffic."

"I wish he would have waited." Skip toyed with the metal clip connecting the clothesline leash to Cleo's collar. All that stood between the cat and freedom was one pull and a turn of the wrist.

"Skip," Vicky's voice reminded him gently.

"If the guy's a creep and a crumb, the cats don't go. Right?"

"Right."

Lynn and her mother were alone in the kitchen. Lynn was so nervous her palms were sweaty. Finally she worked up the courage to make her proposal. "I know who you could get to be Grammer's housekeeper," she said.

"Oh?" Her mother was writing out a list; she was always writing lists.

"Glory and Justin," said Lynn. "Grammer wouldn't kick them out."

Her mother picked up her pen and resumed her list-making. "Don't be absurd, Lynn. We need someone responsible. Not people who'd decide after a couple of weeks to traipse off to a place they poked on a map."

"They only do that in the summer. They're responsible. I know they are. Just ask them, will you?" Lynn pleaded. "Then Grammer won't have to leave."

"I know it's not easy, but it's time you accepted things, dear."

"Do you know what happens to those birds that get caught in the oil?" Lynn said, shaking.

"Lynn, what on earth are you talking about?"

21

❧❧❧

"Vicky. Vick! Your marshmallow's burning," Doug yelled.

"Oh phooey." She blew out the flames and tossed the charred glob. She had been watching the cats tied in the middle of the yard. A small animal of some kind rustled in the underbrush. Rudy and Cleo slunk quietly at the ends of their ropes, straining to find cover and sneak up on their prey. She wished this Dr. Bennett would hurry up. She was weary of feeling like their jailer.

"Vicky! Now you're roasting your stick. Come on, girl, either pay attention or stay away from the fire," her father ordered.

Vicky was discarding her stick when an open jeep stopped on Deerhill Road at the mailbox, then rumbled up their drive. A man stepped down. He wiped his bald head with a handkerchief, then replaced his fishing hat. He must have seen Vicky and her family, but he approached the cats first.

The cats followed him with their eyes. They made no move to retreat or run. Cleo yawned and stretched lazily, pushing back over her haunches.

Doug strode over and extended a hand. "You must be Roger Bennett. Welcome. Beautiful, aren't they?" Dr. Bennett's approval was obvious.

With his ruddy cheeks and slightly dusty attire, he was no one's image of a super-hero, Vicky decided. "They look to me about three, possibly three and a half months old," he said.

"That's our guess," said Doug.

Her father completed the introductions and Nan offered Dr. Bennett dinner. No, he had a sister who lived a few miles away and he was expected there, he said, so they settled down to business.

Right away Skip was signaling his sister that he thought Bennett was okay. Vicky saw the cues, but she persisted with her questions.

Dr. Bennett took it in stride. He had brought pictures of the preserve. Some were of coworkers handling the animals, others showed the types of traps and tags they used to catch and identify them. Dr. Bennett told of hidden cameras and elaborate sensing devices used to study the wildlife as they ranged over the sanctuary.

"In theory bobcats don't need protection. They adapt well to different climates, even on the fringes of urban areas. Man is the bobcat's only natural enemy. With laws to prevent importing endangered cats, furriers have turned to native wildcats. Which is why our bobcat is in such trouble."

Dr. Bennett was working with researchers from several colleges, he explained. "Up to this point we always believed the female cared for her young alone, but we're beginning to find evidence of a limited family or group life." He displayed another set of pictures. "This is a female bob hanging around one of our cages where her litter-mate was trapped.

"We also get involved in restoration projects. Right now we're releasing bobcats in the mountains down in New Jersey."

"That's near where we live!" Skip exclaimed.

Dr. Bennett tucked his fingers in his fishing vest. "Son, I hope you see them when you're out hiking one day."

"All this information you collect — does it mean we can find out what's happened to Rudy and Cleo?" Vicky asked.

Dr. Bennett smiled the same boyish grin they had seen in the magazine article. "We've had a few bobs that were raised by humans. They tend to become regulars at the research stations, since they're not so afraid of human scent. I'll probably be able to send pictures when Cleo has kittens. How's that?"

That clinched it for Vicky.

The next morning the jeep drove up when Dr. Bennett said it would, and he swiftly maneuvered Cleo and Rudy into the wire cages in the back of the vehicle. Vicky was grateful he did not prolong their good-byes.

She stood arm-in-arm with her family. The cats peered through the screening, curious and unknowing. "Quite a group we got here," said Doug, squeezing. The jeep disappeared.

On Sunday the Seymours decorated for their cookout with red and yellow Chinese lanterns and the yard looked positively festive.

162

Grammer had insisted on contributing something. "More like a church supper," she said. "Everybody brings a little and eats a lot. I always enjoyed the idea of church suppers."

She bustled in the kitchen, preparing a relish tray and chocolate cake. At one point Grammer seemed to pale from fatigue, and Justin, waving a dishtowel, chased her out to finish the boiled white icing alone. "Shoo! It's bad luck to have three cooks." And intoning, "Three, three, three," he pretended to perform a lavish ceremony to ward off bad spirits.

Grammer pushed open the swinging door. "I never heard of such a thing."

He had persuaded her to rest — without sacrificing her pride, Lynn noted ruefully. Probably Justin and Glory would have handled the whole pill business better, too. Watching them work together, Grammer and Glory and Justin, she had known what must be done. It was a matter of finding the right moment.

While they were waiting for the charcoal fire, the three families sat around the Seymours' picnic table. Glory strummed her guitar, and Justin told stories of their adventures the two previous summers. Some of it was hilarious — how he had to trade his tools, for instance, for a new tire, then drive back later to reclaim them, and just as he was leaving a second tire blew.

Lynn was keeping an anxious eye on her mother. There was no right moment, she realized — it would never be easy to confront her. She remembered Vicky's advice on speechmaking: She wanted her team to win all right.

At the next lull in the conversation Lynn knew this had to be it. After all the fun and stories she felt out of place.

163

"My mother won't — uh — do this," she began, "so I have to." She thought about Glory's present, the ball of yarn. "It's very hard sometimes to see what else is possible, when you're afraid to."

"Lynn, what is this?" her mother asked.

"Hush," Grammer silenced her.

"Until I realized it was so important to me, I didn't know I could do it." Vicky was right. Once you got rolling it was easier. "Everybody knows what's supposed to happen to Grammer. For some people it may be okay, but not for her. She could stay here if she had someone to stick around and keep an eye on things." She looked directly to Glory and Justin. "What my mother won't ask is if you'd like the job."

Grammer was the first to protest. "Child, you're embarrassing me. I'd rather spend my last days in a fancy rest home in the company of several full sets of false teeth than on my own porch in the company of a babysitter. Why do you think I sent all those other nannies away?"

"But what about the farm?" said Lynn. "You said yourself you were worried about what would happen if you left."

"I am indeed."

"And if you could pick anyone you wanted, you'd choose somebody like Glory and Justin to take care of it. I know you would."

"Yes," said Grammer. "They know how to give a living thing the space it requires. Not many come to the soil with that appreciation." Grammer turned to them. "I always thought Lynn would have the farm after me, but I didn't account for time and infirmities overtaking me. If you were of an inclination to keep your finger pressed to this part of the map, I'd see to it the price was right."

Lynn's mother spoke up. "Gerald and I decided — "

"While I'm able," Grammer barked, "I'll do the deciding."

Then a smile tipped the corners of her mouth, and it widened as a tantalizing thought took over her face. "In fact, I'm offering the farm to you right now for one dollar's rent a year. Payable on my birthday. They'll be the best birthdays I've ever had," she said with glee. "You can move in whenever you're ready."

"Mother Davis — "

"Whenever you're ready," she repeated for Glory and Justin. "However long."

For the first time since he had appeared at the farm Justin was speechless. He tugged at his beard and at his ear. Lynn was imagining the worst. "This comes kind of as a shock. Wow. Glory and I always said we'd know when we found our place. But I wouldn't — we wouldn't" — he corrected himself and reached for Glory's hand — "we wouldn't want you giving us the farm, Mrs. Davis, any more than you want us as babysitters, because it takes away something that's important to both of us.

"If we could work something out to buy the farm fair and square — We have some money put aside and maybe the rest could come out of what we earned when we got it running again — then we'd be interested.

"But not unless you stayed to help us get started. You supply the knowhow, we'll supply the muscle. If you're interested in talking that kind of a bargain," said Justin, "you're on."

This was so much better than Lynn dreamed! "Grammer, do it."

Her words came slowly. "I've lived a lot of years alone. I may be past living with."

"Glory and Justin know what a crab apple you are."

"Crab apple, am I?" Grammer sniffed. Then her face expanded. "As long as that's understood, we have a bargain."

There was a burst of congratulating and hugging all round, except for Lynn's mother. She spoke in the precise, even tones she reserved for when she was particularly angry. "Mother Davis, this is outrageous. I'm calling your father, Lynn, right now. And I want to say I am disappointed that you let yourself become involved in this scheme." She threw a killing look at Justin and Glory. "I'm sure they put you up to this." She snatched her purse and marched for the car.

"Great speech, Lynn," Vicky said afterward. "The first is the hardest."

"Thanks. I'll remember that."

It was an evening like so many others spent on Grammer's porch, enjoying the sweet-scented breezes following a hot day, but tonight held a special feeling for Lynn. Grammer was in her rocker, Glory on the swing with Vicky and Skip, who was humming to a jar of fireflies. Lynn sat on the banister, while Justin sprawled over the steps, elbows resting on the top stair.

Her mother was inside reading, waiting for her father to return her call, and standing behind the screen door every once in a while, suspiciously commenting on how quiet they were.

They had indeed been quiet, though they talked more the blacker it became, as if to make up for losing sight of each other. They hashed over starting up the farm again, perhaps converting some of the acreage to tree farming, as Bob Reidy up the road had done.

At Glory's urging, Grammer reminisced: an hours-long journey by buckboard to see The Old Man of the Mountain when she was a girl in pigtails; the spring when dozens of roofs collapsed under repeated snows; the young college boy at a neighbor's egg stand, who pointed to her dandelion-covered lawn and asked to pick the beautiful yellow flowers. Everyone up and down Deerhill heard about him.

"Hey, Skipper," said Justin, "we could have taken care of your cats, if we'd known."

"That's okay. They're going to a good place. Anyway, I don't think Mrs. Davis — " Poor Skip. He must have realized suddenly who else was listening across the dark.

"Mrs. Davis what?" She wasn't letting it rest.

"I don't think you like bobcats very much," Skip finished.

"Oh no, that's not it." Her rocker went into a spasm of creaking.

It happened again. Mention the Seymours' cats and Grammer disappeared inside herself.

"Then what is it?" Lynn demanded. Always her grandmother had been the one person Lynn relied on not to couch things in pleasant-sounding words and not to discuss something to death if it wasn't worth the breath. "What made you take those kittens to the beach? And what do they have to do with the cove? You said no farmer would keep bobcats. But you did. You had two bobcats. I saw them in the picture album."

The rocker slowed and scraped across the floorboards. It was not a laugh exactly, more a complaint Grammer uttered. "Your Grandfather Davis wasn't much of a farmer, child. His love was the trains.

"I expect you won't think too highly of me after you hear this. The night the kittens were lost I went down to the pond intending to drown them.

"I knew from the first they were bobcats. Yes, I had a pair once. In the end they were nothing but heartache to me. I thought sure the bobs were come back to bedevil me, scratching old sores and bringing us a peck of new troubles." Her voice thinned. "But I couldn't kill them. Not this time. I sat down with them in the sand ... I started losing track, I guess ..."

"You had bobcats?" Glory prodded gently.

"The mother was caught in a trap. Mr. Davis had to shoot her. He saw she was nursing and he found the babies underneath a rotted tree stump. The kits were a love present — our son was newly born. I ignored all the talk I'd heard about wildcats, and I reared them. Spitfires, he called them. Like me." She laughed.

"My, they were beautiful. Running free on the farm. Every moving part worked, including the bob. Not like farm machines, forever needing repair.

"At one time there were wildcats all over. The menfolk out hunting for deer would catch a glimpse of them. Indians, they say, used every part of the bobcat imaginable. They thought the fur was good for cuts, and they'd eat parts for headaches. Even used the cat droppings. To them the wildcat was magical. She could see through stone or wood. And she was a fighter. The toughest there is.

"Something must of happened between their day and

mine. People didn't believe in their magic anymore. After Mr. Davis died, I started getting complaints about the cats, how they were killing off other people's chickens. Not to eat — for sport. I wouldn't believe it until one night my neighbor, the one with the dandelion patch — she was a widow woman, same as I — she convinced me to sit up in her hen yard and watch. Sure enough, my cats come. The two of them, hunting together. I kept waiting, hoping they'd turn back.

"I shot the one cat right there. The other turned tail and run. I waited at home for him till morning, and I shot him, too. It was like taking the heart right out of me. But I had to. The hens were her livelihood.

"They're buried in the cove. I don't recollect the spot anymore. Every place I turned I wondered if this was it.

"Your little bobs brought back a lot. I suppose I thought I'd buried the bad memories ahead of me. But they're like the stones that work up through the New Hampshire dirt. Any farmer knows he has to make a place for them. If he's stubborn, he builds — stone houses and stone walls.

"I felt sorry for those bobs, knowing what was in store. Confinement of some sort. I thought maybe they'd be better off dead."

Lynn stood behind the rocker, wrapping her arms around her grandmother. Each in their own way, they understood Grammer had been talking about herself, a wildcat once.

22

🌱🌱🌱

"My mind's made up, Gerald," Grammer spoke sternly into the phone. She was talking to Lynn's father. She flashed Lynn a "doing fine" gesture, fingers drawn in a circle. Lynn had not seen her looking this excited or happy since they brought Smoke to the farm six years ago.

"What's more," Grammer said, bantering, "I don't take kindly to being called a Communist by your wife. I've voted Republican all my life. This is not like one of those California communes with drugs and people running naked. Good Lord, I'm too old . . ."

There were several more calls over the next two days. Lynn's father talked at length with Glory and Justin, to Lynn, then to Lynn's mother, and to Grammer again, until at last he was willing to go along with the plan. He agreed with Lynn's mother that it probably was not a permanent solution. "But if it makes Grammer happy and keeps her out of a nursing home for a few years," he said, "I'm all for it."

Once the decision was final, Lynn could not help but feel a little sorry for her mother; she seemed very awkward with them, particularly Glory and Justin, and disappeared for the better part of an afternoon. Grammer maintained she had gone shopping for gifts for her club women friends — to show how quaint they still were up in

New Hampshire. But the rented car was parked in the drive, and Lynn guessed her mother had taken a walk.

When she returned she conceded to Lynn that Glory and Justin had demonstrated skill and good sense in caring for her broken elbow, and then she went to work, phoning, making arrangements for Grammer's care until Glory and Justin could come back from Illinois.

Nan slammed the refrigerator. "Done," she said, pleased with herself. She had been cleaning — the last of the eggs, meat, a head of lettuce from the fridge, sugar and raisins from the cupboard. "Skip, will you take a bag of groceries to Mrs. Davis?" she called to the living room.

"I'll do it," said Vicky.

Her mother threw her a surprised look. "Great." Nan handed her the bag. "Tell her to get rid of anything she doesn't want."

Mrs. Davis was sitting on the porch swing beside Lynn. The two of them were bent over a photo album. Vicky waited below the steps until they noticed her. She was feeling uncommonly shy. "We're leaving today."

"Labor Day's a hard day to travel," commented Mrs. Davis.

"Yes, ma'am. This is for you," said Vicky. She stretched out her arms.

"Well, let me have a look." Mrs. Davis peered over her glasses into the bag. "You take those in the kitchen, and put away whatever needs putting away."

Vicky did as she was told, then returned to the porch. She couldn't bring herself to say good-bye.

"Rest your feet, why don't you?" Lynn and her grandmother slid toward one end so Vicky could sit.

The pages of the album turned, one by one. A few of the photographs looked browned, as if they had been held too close to the heat. Some were so old they were cracking.

Vicky was starting to think maybe it was a bad idea to hang around — she didn't know what she expected to find — when Mrs. Davis flipped a page and said to her, "Here's one that ought to be of interest to you." It was a photo of a man, a woman, and a baby, with two cats. If she hadn't known better, she would have said the cats were Rudy and Cleo.

"That's Lynn's Grandfather Davis. And those were the wildcats."

They were real. It was not a ghost story. Vicky was a jumble of feelings, still horrified at what Mrs. Davis had done, yet awed that she possessed the strength. She studied the wrinkled face, fascinated.

Mrs. Davis caught her stare. She patted Vicky. "You run along home now. Your folks will be wanting to leave soon. Remember — when you're out campaigning for President, let them see wildcat in your eye and feel neighbor in your handshake."

Vicky grinned. "I will."

Mrs. Davis and Lynn swayed gently when she stood. "I have your address and phone number," she said to Lynn.

"I have yours."

"See you." Vicky waved. Mrs. Davis and Lynn waved.

Skip was counting license plates as they rode in the back seat of the car. "New Hampshire." Vicky ticked off one more under the N.H. column. "How come it says 'Live Free or Die,' Vick?"

"Every state has a motto." Somewhere in her history books she remembered reading New Hampshire was the first colony to declare independence.

"You want to know what it means?" said Vicky. Skip nodded eagerly. "It means they would rather be dead than not-free. I used to think it was pretty dumb. If you're alive, some day you could run away and get free. But now I think what they meant was that being not-free is the same as being dead, so they might as well die fighting to be free."

"Nobody has to do that today," said Skip.

"Sure they do. Every day. Including you and me."

Skip gave her a quizzical look. Suddenly he flew to the window. "Alaska!"

"A new column for Alaska!" Vicky sang out.

"I haven't gotten any taller," Lynn argued.

"Hush. I want to measure you up." Measuring up meant Grammer stood Lynn in the doorway to the pantry, her back flush with the doorjamb, while Grammer penciled in her height and the date. The doorframe was embellished with little black horizontals marching toward the ceiling. First her father's, which she imagined hidden under the layers of white paint, now hers.

Lynn glanced at the open window. For a moment she thought she heard the moped. But it couldn't be. She would have liked to see Howie one more time, just to say no bad feelings. "See. I stopped growing," said Lynn.

"Never you mind. Some growing you can't see," Grammer crabbed affectionately.

At the last minute Lynn decided to ride with her mother to gas up the rental car for the trip home. She was

173

wearing the navy turtleneck, the sleeve stretched tight over the cast. Her mother noticed when Lynn hopped into the car, but she did not comment.

They were nearly into town when her mother said, "You know, it's a relief to me to have things work out this way. I knew she'd be unhappy in that home in Connecticut, and who wants to be responsible for something like that? Even if we aren't especially close. But I didn't know what else to do. Many other people have had to do it. I was going to grin and bear it, that's all."

Lynn thought about the ball of yarn. She thought about wildcats able to see through wood and stone. "It's okay, Mom. Everything worked out."